THE TOMB OF IRON EYES

Infamous bounty hunter Iron Eyes has the scent of his prey in his nostrils, and is determined to add yet another notch to the gun grip of his famed Navy Colt. Yet the closer he gets to where his outlaw quarry is holed up, the more guns are turned upon him. Refusing to submit to the lethal lead of those who would halt his progress, Iron Eyes forges on towards Cheyenne Falls — and the fate that he knows awaits him . . .

Books by Rory Black
in the Linford Western Library:

THE FURY OF IRON EYES
THE WRATH OF IRON EYES
THE CURSE OF IRON EYES
THE SPIRIT OF IRON EYES
THE GHOST OF IRON EYES
IRON EYES MUST DIE
THE BLOOD OF IRON EYES
THE REVENGE OF IRON EYES
IRON EYES MAKES WAR
IRON EYES IS DEAD
THE SKULL OF IRON EYES
THE SHADOW OF IRON EYES
THE VENOM OF IRON EYES
IRON EYES THE FEARLESS
THE SCARS OF IRON EYES
A ROPE FOR IRON EYES
THE HUNT FOR IRON EYES
MY NAME IS IRON EYES

RORY BLACK

THE TOMB OF IRON EYES

Complete and Unabridged

LINFORD
Leicester

First published in Great Britain in 2015 by
Robert Hale Limited
London

First Linford Edition
published 2016
by arrangement with
Robert Hale
an imprint of The Crowood Press
Wiltshire

*A catalogue record for this book is available
from the British Library.*

ISBN 978–1–4448–3003–3

Published by
F. A. Thorpe (Publishing)
Anstey, Leicestershire

Set by Words & Graphics Ltd.
Anstey, Leicestershire
Printed and bound in Great Britain by
T. J. International Ltd., Padstow, Cornwall

This book is printed on acid-free paper

Dedicated to actor Robert Fuller

Prologue

The distinctive sound of well-maintained spurs rang out in a chilling melody. A moment later the forbidding rider steered his powerful palomino stallion down the high ridge towards the sprawling settlement below. Birds ceased to sing and what animals there were scattered in search of cover. It was as though they sensed the danger which moved through their midst. The aroma of death hung over his emaciated form and seemed to travel with him wherever he went. It was a companion he had grown used to: death had become an old friend.

Familiarity with death provided Iron Eyes with a constant reminder of his own mortality although it was rumoured that he did not fear death because he was already dead. Being considered immortal had its advantages when you lived by the gun. Those who faced his Navy Colts mostly considered themselves already defeated.

His flesh had been brutally scarred by every fight and battle he had found himself embroiled in. He was more akin to a monstrous creature than to a living man.

He was hated by both white and red men alike, but he continued to journey on because there was nowhere for him to settle. Fate had ordained that he would become the best hunter of wanted outlaws and yet his was a hollow existence.

He tossed his mane of long jet-black hair from his face and felt it beat on the shoulders of his battered trail coat.

Just as his flesh bore the scars of his every fight, the trail coat seemed to harbour the marks of each of his many killings. Every drop of dried blood remained upon its tattered fabric like memories for himself and warnings to others. Most of the blood which had soiled his coat had been spilled from his own veins.

His eyes darted all around the area as he steered his mount down through the trees towards the first of the town's many structures. If there was going to be trouble the bounty hunter was ready to meet it head on.

Nothing could slow his pace.

He had been tracking this man for so long he could almost scent him. The crude image of the outlaw was printed upon the folded Wanted poster buried deep in his pocket — the image was branded into his mind. He never forgot a face when it was wanted dead or alive and had a price printed above the picture.

Iron Eyes looked all around him as his mount made its way down towards the edge of the settlement. He drove his spurs into the flanks of his stallion and increased his pace. The palomino began to trot as it reached level ground and approached the town.

His bony left hand teased his long leathers and guided the horse through the trees towards the crude sign that was nailed to a staff. The bounty hunter drew back on his reins and stopped the stallion. He stared down at the marker.

'Cheyenne Falls.' Iron Eyes whispered the name through his sharp teeth before poking a long thin cigar into the corner of his mouth. He scratched his thumbnail across the top of the match and lifted the flame to the end of his cigar. He inhaled deeply and closed his eyes for a brief moment as he savoured the strong tobacco.

He tossed the match aside and opened his bullet-coloured eyes and stared at Cheyenne Falls. He could see enough of the town to understand it. There were three roads leading in and out of the sprawling settlement.

Iron Eyes drew in more smoke and then pulled the long cigar from his scarred lips. There were so many identical towns in the territory. In each of them there was danger for anyone who hunted outlaws for a living.

Cheyenne Falls filled a gulch set between two tree-covered hills. The sun beat down mercilessly across the rooftops of the wooden buildings. Iron Eyes was thoughtful. He had learned the hard way that it paid to evaluate even seemingly peaceful places before riding in with guns blazing.

He raised himself in his stirrups and balanced as he sucked hard on his cigar. The telegraph poles were well hidden by the trees, but he could see them. That was a comfort to the bounty hunter. He lowered himself back down upon the ornate Mexican saddle and tapped his spurs again.

The stallion obeyed its ruthless master.

It walked beyond the marker.

Iron Eyes continued to look about him. His eyes darted back and forth from behind the veil of long strands of sweat-soaked hair. Few men could have looked more hideous to the unsuspecting eyes of any onlookers who might see the bounty hunter's arrival.

Even fewer would have known what to expect from Iron Eyes as he continued to tap his spurs into the bleeding flesh of the high-shouldered animal.

The sun was at its zenith. Iron Eyes glanced up and saw the blinding orb of white light. He then lowered his head again and saw the first of the townsfolk as they went about their daily business.

He continued riding slowly, keeping his gaunt body immobile as he guided the palomino deeper into the town. A score of men were gathered in a circle at the edge of the town. The sound of fighting roosters filled the air, but Iron Eyes showed no interest in cockfights.

The bounty hunter could see the shock and repulsion from the corner of his eyes of both men and women as they set eyes upon his mutilated face. Their gasping terror did not interest him either.

The layout of the buildings became more organized. The deeper he rode into Cheyenne Falls the closer together they got. It was the same in all towns, he thought. Unlike himself it seemed that all other humans needed company. He had no idea why.

He jabbed his spurs into the large stallion's flesh again and it continued to pull on its bit. As with all his previous horseflesh, the palomino wanted to escape the painful spurs, but it was trapped.

There was no escape.

Just like the outlaw he hunted, the stallion was doomed to its fate.

Iron Eyes knew that he was now in the very heart of the town. Buildings suddenly merged together and became busy streets. He teased his long leathers and allowed the stallion to walk into the wide expanse of what he knew had to be the main street.

His eyes darted at every man who wore a gun. He sniffed the air and inhaled the only scent he actually liked.

The aroma of whiskey filled his nostrils. It wafted on the hot midday air from the numerous saloons' open doorways, yet this time Iron Eyes did not stop. The bounty hunter had something more pressing to sort out before he quenched his insatiable thirst.

The lean horseman kept on urging his mount forward past the groups of alarmed townspeople until he found what he was seeking. With a quick jerk of his wrist, he turned the stallion and dismounted as it reached the hitching pole.

Iron Eyes stood like a statue beside the shoulder of the handsome animal and allowed the dust to settle before hitching his reins to the twisted pole and stepping up on to the boardwalk. He paused and surveyed the street like a vulture looking for a tasty body to start ripping apart. The people who had been casually walking in his direction suddenly crossed the wide street to avoid getting too close.

His eyes moved from one saloon to the next as he counted the various drinking holes. The bounty hunter counted fourteen within spitting distance. Every one of them had at least two horses tied up outside whilst their masters drank their fill of the amber rotgut they called whiskey.

He pulled the cigar from his mouth and allowed the grey smoke to filter from between his scarred lips. No detail on the street escaped his cold, calculating eyes and he studied everything.

When he was satisfied he turned to face the sign on the wooden wall. He read it and then leaned down and grabbed the doorknob and twisted it.

He entered the office. His spurs echoed off the wooden interior as he stopped and stared at the desk set below a gun rack with a carbine and scattergun upon it. He lowered his eyes to the man seated behind the desk.

A well-rounded figure looked up, gasped and then rose unsteadily to his feet. The sunlight which had followed the bounty hunter into the office gleamed off the tin star pinned upon the man's chest.

'I'm Sheriff Cord,' he said unsteadily.

Iron Eyes nodded and returned the cigar to his mouth.

'Sheriff,' he said.

Sheriff Josiah Cord looked as though every ounce of colour had been drained from his face as he swallowed hard and gave a nod.

'Who in tarnation are you?' he asked in a vain attempt to sound and look like a confident lawman.

'Iron Eyes.'

The eyebrows rose on Cord's confused face. 'What?'

'My name's Iron Eyes,' the lean figure repeated as his bony hand closed the door behind him. He took a step closer to the ashen-faced lawman. 'I'm a bounty hunter.'

It was as though every ounce of courage had suddenly drained out of the star-packer. Cord nervously sat back down and rubbed his face. Yet no matter how hard he rubbed his jowls he could not stop his eyes staring at the hideous sight before him. Cord had never seen anything, that was not already dead, that looked as bad as Iron Eyes.

The sheriff looked at the gaunt bounty hunter. The grips of the two Navy Colts protruded from behind his belt buckle and pointed straight across the desk at him.

'So you're a bounty hunter, are you?' he managed to say without stammering.

Iron Eyes advanced another step. 'Yep. Maybe you've heard of me?'

Cord shook his head. 'Nope, I ain't ever heard about you. I'd have remembered you sure enough. You ain't the kind of critter a person could forget in a hurry.'

Iron Eyes was not certain, but it sounded as though he had been insulted.

'You got a bad notion about bounty hunters?' he asked.

Cord shook his head. 'We don't tend to attract many of your profession to Cheyenne Falls.'

The bounty hunter inhaled deeply and then pulled the cigar from his mouth and stepped to the window. His narrowed eyes stared out into the street as smoke slowly drifted from his mouth.

'I'm looking for a wanted varmint, Sheriff,' Iron Eyes said as his left hand disappeared into his deep trail-coat pocket and produced a Wanted poster. He pulled it out, shook it and handed it to the lawman. 'You seen this man?'

Cord took the poster and flattened it out on his ink blotter. He studied the crude photographic image and scratched his unshaven face.

'Nope, can't say I have,' he answered.

Faster than the sheriff had ever seen anyone move before, Iron Eyes turned on his heels and snatched the poster from the sheriff's desk.

'Are you sure?' Iron Eyes asked coldly.

Cord looked up at the face which loomed over him. He had never seen such a face in all his days. He tried to smile, but no amount of forcing could make his face obey. He raised his hands and meekly shrugged.

'Honest, I ain't seen that critter,'

Cord managed to reply as he felt sweat trace down his spine. 'Are you sure he's in Cheyenne Falls?'

Iron Eyes straightened up and stared at the poster in his hand. His eyes narrowed as they glared at the image printed upon the paper.

'Joe Corrigan,' he read aloud. 'He's wanted dead or alive for double murder and bank robbery. It says here that he's worth $1,000.'

Cord had never before encountered a bounty hunter. If Iron Eyes was an example of the profession, he did not care to meet any others.

'I asked you if Corrigan is in Cheyenne Falls, Iron Eyes.' He asked again. 'Well, is he?'

Iron Eyes folded the paper and poked it back down into his pocket. The sound of loose bullets filled the small office. The lean bounty hunter blew a long line of smoke at the floor and then stared into the sheriff's eyes.

'Corrigan had a few days start on me, Sheriff,' Iron Eyes said as his fists clenched. 'I lost him back at Adobe Wells and rode across country to head him off. By my figuring he's headed in this direction.'

'But you don't know if he's even headed here or not, do you?' Cord said.

The bullet-coloured eyes burned into the seated lawman. He stepped closer to the fat sheriff.

'He's either here already or he's headed here, Sheriff,' Iron Eyes replied. 'There ain't no other place within twenty miles of Cheyenne Falls.'

Cord cleared his throat. 'How can you be so sure he's riding here?'

The bounty hunter turned and walked back to the door. He grabbed its handle and pulled it towards him. He then paused briefly and stared at the sweating sheriff.

'I know he's headed here,' he repeated.

'But how can you be so sure?' Cord asked.

There was a long pause as the bounty hunter drew smoke into his lungs. Then the bullet-coloured eyes stared straight at the lawman.

'Because I'm Iron Eyes,' he said. 'That's how.'

1

Iron Eyes stepped down from the boardwalk, pulled his reins free and led the palomino stallion across the street towards one of the many saloons that were dotted along its length. For midday Cheyenne Falls had grown unusually quiet. The townsfolk who normally paraded its length had paused and were huddled in stores along the main street. Many pairs of eyes watched the tall thin figure as he walked towards the saloon. The silvery tinkle of his spurs seemed to warn of disaster.

The gaunt bounty hunter glanced at a small building set halfway along the street. He did not have to read the large sign which had been erected above its doorway to know what it was. Every telegraph wire converged at a high pole and then ran down into the telegraph office.

Iron Eyes looked around him as he pulled the tall palomino towards the saloon. He watched the men, women and children who watched him. He returned their gaze with an icy stare towards the saloon and looked through its two large windows. They were set to either side of the welcoming swing doors and offered him a good view of what was behind him in their reflective surface.

Iron Eyes could see the sheriff's reflection as well as countless others watching his every move. Over the years that simple trick had saved him from being back-shot many times.

The name of the freshly painted drinking hole was 'The Lucky Lizard' but it was not that which attracted him. It was the water trough set just before a twenty-foot-long hitching pole. He knew the powerful stallion was thirsty just like its master.

Iron Eyes reached the pole, secured his long leathers and then stepped up under the well-shaded porch overhang.

He faced the street and watched as the stallion drank. Iron Eyes then swung on his heels and pushed the swing doors apart with one hand whilst his other rested close to his gun grips.

For a brief moment Iron Eyes simply stood as the swing doors rocked on their hinges behind his wide back. His eyes darted around the room at every face in turn.

Then the tall emaciated figure walked across the saloon towards the long mahogany counter. The saloon fell into silence as each of its patrons caught sight of the man with the haunting spurs.

None of them had ever seen anyone who looked as horrific or dangerous as Iron Eyes before. His gun grips poked ominously out from his flat belly from the belt buckle they were nestled behind. Choking cigar smoke hung in the air as the tall bounty hunter cut a path through it.

With each long stride patrons finished their drinks and hastily departed into the street. It was like a stampeding herd of mavericks. By the time Iron Eyes reached the counter only the bartender remained in the Lucky Lizard.

The wide-eyed bartender stood open-mouthed as Iron Eyes rested one hand on the counter and the other on a gun grip. There was a long silence before the man finally managed to ask his only remaining customer:

'What'll it be, stranger?'

'Whiskey,' Iron Eyes said drily as he pulled a golden coin from his shirt pocket and placed it on the stained wooden surface of the counter. 'An unopened bottle.'

The man nodded and reached behind him to a shelf where a score of whiskey bottles were stacked. He grabbed one of them and then placed it down before the bounty hunter.

'Is that OK?' the bartender asked.

The bullet-coloured eyes studied the bottle, which still had its seal across the cork. Iron Eyes looked up at the nervous bartender.

'It'll do,' he answered.

The bartender reached for a thimble glass when Iron Eyes grabbed the bottle up.

'I don't need no glass,' he whispered.

The terrified bartender looked on as Iron Eyes pulled the cork from the bottle with his teeth, spat it at a spittoon and then walked to one of the corners and sat down behind a card table. He lifted the bottle to his lips and took a long swig from the long clear glass neck. He did not lower it until half of its contents had disappeared down his throat.

'You must be mighty thirsty, stranger,' the bartender said nervously.

The bounty hunter nodded.

The bartender began to shake as the icy stare continued to drill into him. Every instinct told him to run for his life, but that would require a courage he did not possess.

Iron Eyes noticed his cigar had gone

out. He struck a match with his thumbnail and lifted it back to the remainder of the black weed gripped between his teeth. He exhaled and blew his match out. 'You seen a varmint around here named Joe Corrigan in the last couple of days?'

The question was like a meat cleaver. It hit the bartender between the eyes. He nervously stammered.

'Joe Corrigan?' the bartender repeated before he started to polish glasses and wipe the table down.

Iron Eyes placed the whiskey bottle on the table and rose back up from his chair. He started to walk across the sawdust back towards the counter. With every step the spurs played their haunting tune.

'That's right,' he growled. 'Joe Corrigan. Have you seen him in town?'

The bartender continued to polish glasses.

'I'm not sure I've heard the name before, stranger.'

Iron Eyes reached the counter and

placed his boot heel on the brass rail. He stared through the rising cigar smoke at the terrified man. The bartender was lying, but the bounty hunter was not sure exactly why.

'You've heard the name before,' he whispered. 'I'd bet my scalp on that, friend.'

The bartender was shaking so hard the glass he had been polishing fell from his grip and smashed upon the floor at his feet. He attempted to keep his eyes from the bounty hunter, but Iron Eyes grabbed his shoulder and swung him around violently to face him.

The bartender felt the cold steel of a Navy Colt push up into his throat. Then Iron Eyes leaned close and stared into the eyes of the frightened man.

'Where is he?' Iron Eyes growled.

'I don't know,' the bartender croaked.

'You're a pretty bad liar,' Iron Eyes said. 'Protecting a wanted killer could see you end up as dead as he'll surely be when I catch up with him.'

'I ... I don't know him,' the bartender insisted.

Iron Eyes did not say another word. He cocked his gun and watched as the nervous man's eyes widened. Then he pulled the six-shooter away from the bartender's throat and trained it at the table. Without even turning his attention from the man in his grip Iron Eyes fired his weapon.

The whiskey bottle shattered into a million fragments. Glass floated into the air as the amber contents soaked the green baize and then dripped on to the floor.

'That could have been your head, mister,' Iron Eyes said as his thumb dragged the hammer back again.

The bartender winced as the hot steel of the smoking gun barrel was pressed back into his throat.

'Please don't shoot me,' the bartender whimpered. 'I'll tell you where he is. I'll tell you everything you wanna know. Just don't kill me.'

Iron Eyes released his grip and

allowed the bartender to compose his shaking frame.

'Where is he?' he drawled.

The bartender swallowed hard. 'He's not in town. He rode for Devil's Canyon with two mules laden down with provisions.'

Iron Eyes reeled back on his heels at the unexpected news he had just dragged from the terrified man. His scarred eyebrows rose as he released his hammer and eased it back down on to the body of his still smoking weapon.

'Devil's Canyon?' He repeated the unfamiliar name.

'That's where he's gone.' The bartender picked up the napkin and wiped the sweat from his face. He nodded and then dragged another bottle from the shelf. 'Joe lit out hardly an hour after he'd got into town. He bought a new nag to replace his spent one. Looking at you I can see why he was in such an almighty hurry.'

Iron Eyes grabbed the bottle from the bartender and pulled its cork.

'Where in tarnation is Devil's Canyon? I've never heard of the damn place.'

'It's beyond the hills,' the bartender answered. 'I'm told it's out in the desert someplace.'

'Why'd he head there?' Iron Eyes asked.

The bartender leaned forward. 'I'm told there are rich pickings out there in the canyon. Cheyenne gold mines filled with nuggets as big as a man's fist. A fortune for anyone that's lucky enough to find it. That's why he's headed out there.'

Iron Eyes took a swig from the bottle. 'What in tarnation is a damn killer doing looking for gold mines?'

The bartender shook his head. 'Him and his brothers have been looking for them ancient Cheyenne gold mines for more than five years. The way he rode through here I guess he figured that having you on his tail was a good time to resume his former career.'

'He wasn't feared of me?' Iron Eyes wondered. 'He knows I'm on his tail yet he went hunting gold?'

The bartender gave a nervous nod of his head. 'Looks that way, but I reckon having you hunting him sure spurred him on. I never seen Joe look as troubled as he was when he left town.'

Iron Eyes pushed the bottle to the shaking man.

'Have yourself a drink,' he said.

'Much obliged,' the bartender said as he picked up a glass and filled it with whiskey. 'You intending to follow him?'

Iron Eyes was about to answer when the swing doors were flung apart and a large burly man entered the Lucky Lizard. He stood watching Iron Eyes with a cocked scattergun in his hands.

The bartender lowered the glass before the whiskey had reached his lips.

'Holy Smoke,' he gasped.

Iron Eyes kept the gun in his hand as he looked over his shoulder at the large figure.

'Who is that?' he asked.

'That's Big Dan McGraw,' the bartender said. 'He's one of Joe

Corrigan's boys.'

Iron Eyes swung around and faced McGraw. He inhaled deeply and spat the cigar from his mouth as he straightened up.

For a moment neither McGraw nor Iron Eyes spoke. They just eyed one another up and down. Then McGraw took a step forward. Sawdust rose from the pressure of his large boot as it hammered down on to the floorboards.

'I just heard that a stinking bounty hunter had ridden into Cheyenne Falls,' McGraw boomed. 'I got me a feeling that I've found him.'

Iron Eyes lowered his head.

'I'm the one you're looking for,' he said. 'I'm the bounty hunter. I'm gonna find and kill Joe Corrigan.'

The fuse had been ignited. McGraw suddenly burst into action and lifted his massive scattergun. Both barrels were aiming at the gaunt figure.

Yet as soon as his bullet-coloured eyes saw the large trigger finger move, Iron Eyes threw himself to the floor.

Buckshot carved a massive hole in the bar as it flew past the bounty hunter. Wooden debris flew up into the air as the bartender dived for cover.

Iron Eyes hit the floor hard and fanned his gun hammer.

Blood sprayed from McGraw as the bounty hunter's bullets tore through him. He dropped the massive scatter-gun and fell to his knees. He clawed at his holstered gun as Iron Eyes fired another bullet into his large frame.

McGraw fell on to his face. Blood encircled his massive form and spread out across the sawdust towards the bounty hunter.

Iron Eyes slowly rose to his feet and dusted himself off as he strode to the deathly silent McGraw. 'Is this varmint wanted, barkeep?'

'I don't rightly know,' the bartender answered as he peered over the massive gash in the mahogany counter. 'Why'd you wanna know?'

Iron Eyes shook the spent casings from his gun and then scooped fresh bullets from his deep trail-coat pocket. He started to reload the smoking gun. His ice-cold eyes darted between the living man and the corpse.

'If there ain't no bounty on his stinking head then I've wasted one hell of a lot of expensive lead killing him,' he said bitterly. 'Killing honest folks is pitiful. There ain't no profit in it.'

2

Sheriff Josiah Cord eased his body reluctantly from his office chair and glanced through the door across the wide street at the Lucky Lizard just as Iron Eyes emerged with the smoking Navy Colt in one hand and a bottle of whiskey in the other. Cord stopped in his tracks on the boardwalk and felt his mouth go dry as the bounty hunter glanced up at him. For the lawman it was like looking into the face of Satan himself.

Iron Eyes rammed the gun into his belt beside its twin and then stepped down on to the sandy street. He tugged the long leathers free of the hitching pole and then touched his brow to the sheriff.

Somehow Cord managed to smile at the hideous sight. Iron Eyes led his tall stallion down the street towards the largest structure in Cheyenne Falls. Only when the bounty hunter had walked far away from the saloon did Cord summon the nerve to cross from his office to the Lucky Lizard to investigate.

Iron Eyes could see every one of the town's people sheltering in various stores as he made his way unhindered down the centre of the main thorough-fare. He aimed his boots at the tall structure set a hundred yards from the livery stable.

The sign was simple yet large.

It read 'Hotel' in bold, newly painted letters across its façade. The bounty hunter glanced up at its four windows which stretched the length of the veranda and then lowered his head and studied the front of the building. A large double door with glass panes was set between windows with shutters. The doors were wide open.

Iron Eyes took that as an invitation.

He looped his reins over a hitching rail and tied a secure knot to prevent the stallion from bolting away. He then slid the bottle of amber whiskey into one of his deep trail-coat pockets and walked up the four steps to the doorway.

He could see the ornate decoration within the foyer of the hotel and moved out of the baking afternoon sun into it. His spurs rang out a sorrowful tune as he strode across the carpeted floor towards the desk and a pale-skinned man who looked as though he had never once allowed the sun to touch his sickly flesh.

The man was no more than five feet tall and reminded Iron Eyes of a small animal. He seemed to have been trying to grow a moustache, but as with so many men of his frail build it did not flourish.

Iron Eyes bore down on the desk and the man who stood behind it. The bounty hunter rested a hand upon it.

The small clerk looked up into the devilish features of Iron Eyes. He tried to appear unconcerned, but the sight which greeted his curious eyes was too much for him. His eyes rolled up and disappeared under his lids. He took a sharp intake of breath and then collapsed in a heap beside his chair.

Bewildered, Iron Eyes leaned over the desk and stared down at the unconscious clerk.

He had never seen anyone faint before and it troubled the gaunt bounty hunter. For a few moments Iron Eyes simply stood watching the clerk as another more sturdy man appeared from behind a large drape.

Ben Bevis had owned the hotel for nearly ten years yet in all of that time he too had never set eyes upon anything like Iron Eyes.

Bevis looked at the haunting figure on the opposite side of the desk and felt his heart quicken. He cleared his throat and stepped over the clerk. He turned the register around and dipped a pen into an inkwell before handing it to his new guest.

'My name's Ben Bevis,' the owner of

the hotel said. 'I own this fine hotel. Best in the territory.'

Iron Eyes glanced around at the fine surroundings and shrugged. 'It's mighty fancy, Bevis.'

'I reckon you'll want a room, stranger,' he noted. 'Just make your mark here.'

The bony hand of the bounty hunter took the pen and scrawled his name across the book where Bevis pointed. Iron Eyes then placed the pen back in the inkwell and watched as Bevis swung the book back around so that he could read the signature.

'Mr Iron Eyes?' he said in a faltering tone.

'Yep.'

Bevis pulled a square of white lace from his pocket and mopped his brow.

'How long do you want the room for?' Bevis plucked a key from the wall where a score of other keys hung from hooks. He then tossed it on to the pages of the open ledger.

'Just tonight,' Iron Eyes said as he

continued to stare down at the clerk on the floor beside Bevis's feet. 'I got me a wanted outlaw to hunt down and kill.'

Bevis swallowed hard as he felt the hairs on the nape of his neck start to rise under his collar.

'That'll be two dollars,' Bevis informed him.

Iron Eyes pulled two silver dollars from his shirt pocket and placed them on the book as he picked up the key. Iron Eyes was about to walk off when he paused and pointed at the clerk with a long bony finger.

'What's wrong with that critter?' he asked.

Bevis looked down with a frown. 'He's my sister's son. His name is Gerald. He tends to faint like that when he sees something that scares him.'

'What scared him?'

'You did,' Bevis said. 'Gerald ain't used to setting eyes on real men like yourself. You're a lot more rugged than he's used to looking at.'

Iron Eyes nodded. 'Damn pity the

outlaws I hunt ain't all afflicted like him. It sure would make my life a whole lot easier.'

Bevis grinned. 'Shall I have your horse taken to the livery for you?'

Iron Eyes nodded again and tossed another couple of coins to the hotel owner.

'Much obliged. Have him watered and grained,' he said as Bevis caught the coins in his sweating hands.

Bevis touched his temple. 'I sure will. Room six. You'll find it at the top of the stairs on the right. I'm sure you'll like it, Mr Iron Eyes.'

The sound of the haunting melody rang out from his spurs as Iron Eyes walked to the wide staircase and proceeded up its carpeted steps towards the landing.

Iron Eyes reached the landing, stopped and produced another long thin cigar from his pocket. He gripped it with his sharp teeth and struck a match. He raised the flickering flame to his cigar.

His bullet-coloured eyes looked back down at Bevis and his pathetic nephew. There was something about Bevis which troubled the infamous bounty hunter.

That Something would continue to gnaw at his innards until he recalled what it was. He inhaled the smoke and then blew the match out. He moved to the room door, slid the key into its lock and opened it. The room was better than most hotel rooms he had rented in the past, but it had one drawback.

Iron Eyes walked across the room and stared out of its window at the veranda.

To him windows served only two purposes. Neither of them was any good to his way of thinking.

One was to look out of and the other was to shoot in through. The veranda offered any hopeful assassin a real easy way of taking a potshot at him.

Iron Eyes thoughtfully chewed on the cigar as his bony hands pulled the whiskey bottle from his pocket. He tossed the bottle into the centre of the bed and walked to the room door. He removed the key, closed the door and then reinserted the key into the lock. He turned it until he heard it lock securely.

He stared through the cigar smoke and removed his trail coat. The sound of the many bullets contained in its pockets made the only noise within the room as he tossed it on to a chair.

He sat down on the bed and drew more smoke into his lungs.

Where did he know Bevis from?

The question kept tormenting him.

3

Ben Bevis led the palomino stallion into the livery stable and instructed the blacksmith to water and grain the powerful mount. He then walked across to the telegraph office and entered. The operator rose from his chair and rested his elbow on his desk and looked at Bevis.

'Ain't seen you in here for the longest while, Ben,' he said as he licked the tip of his pencil and hovered above a large white pad of notepaper.

Bevis faked a grin and handed a scrap of paper to the telegraph operator. 'Send this for me, Sam.'

The man seemed to look at the paper without reading it. He just totted up how much the message would cost the hotel owner.

'That'll come to eighty cents,' he said.

Bevis nodded in agreement and handed a dollar to him. 'That'll be fine, Sam. Here. Keep the change.'

'That's mighty fine of you, Ben.' The operator smiled. 'I'm much obliged.'

Bevis left the office and crossed the street. He rushed back to the hotel.

The telegraph operator sat down and started to tap out the message. As his finger beat steadily he read out the message aloud.

To Drako Sharp, Coleman City. Iron Eyes is in hotel. Get here fast. Signed Ben Bevis.

The bounty hunter had been quite correct about windows. They did only serve two real purposes to him and one of those purposes was to look out from.

Iron Eyes moved away from the lace drape. He returned to his bed and sat down again.

'Why would Bevis go to the telegraph office?' he asked himself thoughtfully. 'That critter is up to something and I don't like the idea of not knowing what it is.'

He then thought of another use for a window. He stood up, walked back across the room and opened it. He then poked his leg out on to the veranda and followed it into the sunlight.

Iron Eyes moved like a panther across the veranda until he reached a flight of steps which led down into the alley beside the hotel. The tall thin figure ran down the steps and then moved back towards the street.

He crossed the wide road and entered the telegraph office swiftly. As he closed the door his mane of limp long hair hung over his scarred features until his skeletal fingers combed them back.

Sam looked up and then gasped. He could not conceal his horror and shock at the hideous apparition. His shaking arms rose into the air.

'Please don't shoot,' he begged.

Iron Eyes looked at him blankly.

'I'm not going to rob you,' he said. 'All I want is information.'

The telegraph operator sighed with

relief and dropped his arms. He rubbed his temple anxiously.

'Thank the Lord. I thought I was a goner for a moment when I saw them guns you got tucked in your belt,' the telegraph operator stammered before adding, 'What information do you want?'

Iron Eyes stared across the distance between them.

'What did Bevis want in here?' he bluntly enquired.

'He just wanted a wire sent,' Sam retorted as his eyes remained fixed upon the gleaming guns barely hidden by the belt buckle of the bounty hunter.

'What was the message?' Iron Eyes asked ominously as he rested the knuckles of his left hand upon the desk and glared at the frail figure.

The ancient operator stood and rubbed his unshaven jaw as he moved to the desk and looked hard at the bounty hunter. He knew the company rules for privacy. They were branded into his soul, but he also sensed that the strange man before him was not a figure to be subdued by rules.

'You know I ain't allowed to tell you that, friend. It's private. The company has a whole bunch of rules,' Sam said fearfully. 'It's more than my job's worth to go gabbing about messages to strangers.'

Iron Eyes pulled out a freshly minted ten-dollar banknote and placed it on the desk. His bullet-coloured eyes watched the telegraph man starting to be tempted. Iron Eyes then peeled another bill and placed it on top of the first one.

'Twenty dollars buys a lot in these parts,' the bounty hunter whispered before he laid a third banknote down. 'Thirty dollars buys even more.'

A bead of sweat ran down the side of the old man's face as he stared at the three ten-dollar bills. Without uttering a reply, Sam placed the scrap of paper Bevis had given him only moments earlier in front of Iron Eyes. He slid the bills off the desk and pocketed them as

Iron Eyes read the brief message.

'I never told you anything, stranger,' Sam said. 'I never broke no company rules.'

Iron Eyes nodded. 'That's right, friend.'

Sam pulled a pipe from his pocket and placed the stem in his mouth. 'As long as we understand one another.'

'Thanks,' Iron Eyes said wryly.

Sam turned and looked at the bounty hunter.

'For what?' he asked before striking a match and holding its flame over his pipe bowl. 'I don't know what you're talking about.'

The bounty hunter moved to the office window and glanced out into the dusty street. Tumbleweed rolled down its length as the breeze whipped up tufts of dust which danced like desert nymphs.

'Will you let me know if Bevis gets a reply from this Drako Sharp?' Iron Eyes asked without taking his eyes off the hotel. 'I'll be generous.'

Sam cleared his throat and then tapped his few remaining teeth with the pipe stem.

'I surely will,' he replied before adding, 'Ain't my fault if strangers like yourself happen to see private telegraph messages before I can deliver them.'

Iron Eyes nodded and left the office as secretly as he had entered it. He raced back to the alley beside the hotel and then mounted the steps back up to the veranda. Within seconds he was back in his hotel room.

He placed a cigar between his teeth and closed the window. A smile etched his horrific features as he sparked a match with his thumbnail and raised its flame to the end of the long cigar. The bounty hunter filled his lungs and reflected.

After a few seconds smoke trailed from his lips.

'This is getting mighty interesting,' Iron Eyes whispered before moving towards the bed and the waiting whiskey bottle.

He was about to pick up the amber liquor when the door shook as something knocked upon its surface.

Iron Eyes twisted on his heels and drew one of his Navy Colts and cocked its hammer. His eyes narrowed and he stared at the door.

It shook as it was pounded once more.

'Who is it?' he growled.

There was no reply; only a third violent rapping upon the door. Like a tiger moving towards its prey, Iron Eyes began to approach the door.

'What do you want?' he snarled whilst keeping his gun trained on the door. 'Answer or I'll fire. I ain't joking.'

The door rocked again as it was thumped a fourth time.

'I warned you,' Iron Eyes yelled. He squeezed his trigger and sent a bullet through the top of the door. A shaft of sunlight streamed in through the bullet hole and the bounty hunter heard the unmistakable sound of boots running away from the door.

He raced to the door, turned its key and opened it. Sawdust still floated in the air as Iron Eyes stepped out on to the landing. Whoever it was that had been pounding on his door was now running down the lushly carpeted staircase.

Iron Eyes hurried to the head of the stairs, looked down and just caught sight of a shadow as someone raced out of the foyer into the street. The bounty hunter looked down at the desk in search of either Bevis or his hapless nephew.

There was nobody there.

Iron Eyes rested a hand on the railing and leapt over it. He fell down into the foyer of the hotel and rushed to the wide-open doorway. He followed on to the boardwalk, the Navy Colt in his hand, a bullet carved through the dry air and tore a lump of wood from its frame.

The bounty hunter shook the smouldering sawdust from his face and then cautiously peered around at the mutilated wood. There was no sign of the shooter.

Iron Eyes raised his free arm and ran his sleeve across his face. He spat and then spotted the swing doors of one of the saloons opposite swinging on their hinges.

A ferocity swelled inside his lean form.

Whoever it was that had taken a potshot at him had crossed the street and entered the saloon. Iron Eyes inhaled and then began walking straight towards the very same saloon that he had entered earlier.

Those who had once more started to venture along the street when their courage had returned to them suddenly took flight again. Yet the bounty hunter did not see any of them.

His attention was on the two-storey saloon.

Nothing else mattered.

His bullet-coloured eyes darted to each of the Lucky Lizard's windows and doorway. The tall gaunt bounty hunter moved silently apart from the sound of his spurs. He strode towards the swing doors with one of his guns gripped in his bony hand.

He did not pause as he stepped up on to the boardwalk and pushed the swing doors inwards with his free hand. He continued to walk across the sawdust-covered floor towards the bartender as his eyes scrutinized the seven faces that registered amazement at his sudden appearance.

Iron Eyes did not stop until he reached the counter. Then he raised the gun and aimed at the one face which was not watching him.

'Did that varmint just run in here, barkeep?' he drawled.

The bartender gave a nod and began to step away from the emaciated bounty hunter. The sound of the haunting spurs filled the silence as Iron Eyes walked away from the counter and closed in on the seated man.

'Why'd you shoot at me?' Iron Eyes asked.

The man's face was hidden by his battered Stetson. He sat at a liquor-stained card table in a position which would have been better suited to a church pew.

Iron Eyes stopped and then he suddenly kicked out at the table. It flew from in front of the seated man and crashed into the wall.

'I'll ask you again,' he snarled. 'Why'd you shoot at me?'

Finally the man lifted his head and stared up at the ominous figure who was looming over him with his gun trained straight at his chest.

'I didn't shoot at you,' the man defiantly said.

'Your gun tells a different story,' Iron Eyes informed the man.

The man leaned back on his chair. 'How can a dumb six-shooter tell you anything?'

'The smoke trailing from your holster tells me that you just fired that gun.'

Iron Eyes spat venomously. 'The barkeep tells me that you only just ran in here. You're the only bastard in this saloon who didn't have himself a drink before him. Now are you gonna spill the beans?'

The man started to twitch. 'I don't even know who you are. Why would I shoot at you?'

'Maybe you're suicidal.' Iron Eyes smiled and watched as the seated man began to slide his hand up his pants leg towards his holstered weapon.

The man moved his hand faster.

Suddenly a white flash exploded from the barrel of the Navy Colt. The bullet travelled the five-feet distance and carved a hole through the man's hand and leg.

Flesh and bones shattered as the man screamed and went to rise. Iron Eyes's boot prevented it; the bounty hunter pressed his heel into the groin of the injured man as blood squirted from the horrific wound.

'You sure cry a lot,' Iron Eyes said as

his thumb pulled back on his hammer and cocked his gun again. He pushed the hot barrel into the brow of his trapped target. 'Now tell me the truth before I kill you.'

'I was given a note with a hundred bucks in it,' the man stammered as his hands tried to stem the bleeding. 'I don't know who sent it. It told me to kill you.'

Iron Eyes lowered his leg and stared at the pitiful creature before him.

'You ought to find a new line of work,' he advised. 'You sure ain't much good at this 'un.'

The eyes of the injured man watched as the bounty hunter turned and began to walk back through the stunned onlookers towards the swing doors. His eyebrows furrowed as his bloody hand clawed at his gun grip and drew it from his holster.

'Die, you bastard!' he screamed as he cocked his gun.

With the speed of a whirlwind, Iron Eyes pirouetted and fired. His deadly shot was fast and accurate. His bullet-coloured eyes coldly observed the head of the seated man jolt back with the impact of the shot.

Droplets of crimson trailed the dead figure as he and the chair crashed on to the floor. The blood began to pool before being absorbed by the sawdust.

Every one of the saloon's patrons wanted to run, but they knew that any sudden movement might cause the skeletal figure to turn his gun upon them.

For a few seemingly endless seconds Iron Eyes stared at his handiwork.

There was not a hint of emotion in his scarred face.

'He should have quit while he was ahead,' he drawled.

4

The aromatic scent of pipe tobacco smoke filled the flared nostrils of Iron Eyes as he reached the hotel landing and moved towards his room. He halted and stared with calculating eyes towards his open room door before drawing both his Navy Colts from his belt. He knew that his spurs would betray him as he reached the room, but the closer he got the more familiar the scent became.

His tall lean frame paused momentarily.

'Is that you, Sheriff?' he enquired.

'It's me, Iron Eyes,' Josiah Cord replied.

Iron Eyes entered the room and stared at the lawman sitting upon the edge of the bed. He pushed both his guns back into his belt and walked back to where his bottle waited.

'Drink?' he asked Cord.

The lawman gave a nod of his head. 'Yep.'

Iron Eyes handed the bottle to the sheriff and then lifted his long coat off the chair and put it on. He watched as Cord removed the cork and took a swig of the fiery brew and then handed it back.

'Much obliged,' the lawman said as he puffed on his pipe.

Iron Eyes lifted the bottle to his own lips and drained a third of its contents before taking a breath. The bounty hunter walked around and faced the sheriff.

'What you want, Sheriff?' he eventually asked.

Cord looked up at the gruesome face. 'I heard the shooting and figured it had to be you killing another critter.'

'I only kill two types of critter,' Iron Eyes explained as he returned the whiskey bottle to the older man. 'Folks that have bounty on their heads and the critters that try to kill me.'

Cord lowered the bottle from his mouth. 'We hauled Big Dan off to the funeral parlour and now it seems like you killed another witless critter.'

'I ain't denying it,' Iron Eyes said bluntly. 'I just shot a man dead for trying to kill me over in the Lucky Lizard. Don't know who he was or who hired him but he sure was bad at killing.'

'Was he any good at dying?'

'He was real good at dying, Sheriff.'

Cord stood and handed the bottle back to the tall bounty hunter. He moved to the door and then glanced back at the strange creature called Iron Eyes.

'How many more folks you figure on killing in Cheyenne Falls, Iron Eyes?' he asked.

Iron Eyes shrugged. 'That depends on how many others have been hired to kill me.'

The pipe smoke circled Cord as he nodded. 'Just remember which side of the law you stand on, Iron Eyes. I'd hate for you to become the same as the critters you hunt.'

'It's a fine line, Sheriff,' Iron Eyes noted.

'Try not to cross it, son.' Cord smiled and then left the room.

Iron Eyes rubbed his jaw. He drained what was left of the whiskey, tossed the bottle on to the bed and walked back into the corridor. He could hear the footsteps of the lawman as Cord left the hotel before he locked the room door. He slid the key into his pants pocket and then pulled the collar of his trail coat up around his neck.

Slowly the bounty hunter walked to the staircase and started to descend towards the foyer. His spurs jangled with each deliberate step he took as his eyes spotted Bevis sitting behind the desk reading a newspaper.

Bevis glanced up at him as he reached the foyer, and smiled. Iron Eyes shook his mane of long black hair off his face and gave the hotel owner an icy glare.

As the tall emaciated figure walked out on to the boardwalk he wondered about the wire Bevis had sent to Coleman City again.

Whoever Drako Sharp was, he had been summoned by Bevis to come to this remote settlement. The tall bounty hunter wondered why. As far as he could recall there were no Wanted posters on anyone with such an unusual name. His mind drifted to Big Dan McGraw and wondered why the massive man had taken it upon himself to try to kill him. Corrigan seemed to have a lot of friends or maybe the outlaw just paid them for killing anyone who dared get close to him.

His narrowed eyes darted to where the sun was finally setting. The sky was on fire and the blue heavens were rippled with scarlet waves. His bony fingers pulled a long, twisted cigar from one of his bullet-filled pockets and rammed it between his teeth.

Iron Eyes scratched a match down a wooden upright and cupped its flame just below the cigar which hung from his scarred lips. He sucked in smoke and was thoughtful as he stared over his hands.

Cheyenne Falls was a lot more dangerous than he had first considered. There seemed to be danger everywhere within its boundaries.

Iron Eyes wanted to ride out after the outlaw Joe Corrigan right now, but knew that his sturdy palomino stallion needed time to regain its intrepid strength after the gruelling ride to this town. Even though Iron Eyes knew it was a mistake, he would have to remain in Cheyenne Falls until dawn.

The desert was no place to ride across with a weary mount, he silently told himself. He would have to endure whatever came his way through the hours of darkness.

The infamous bounty hunter walked towards the setting sun, leaving a trail of cigar smoke in his wake. Cheyenne Falls was a town with many secrets, he thought. It was a town with too many guns and so far two of them had tried to kill him.

Yet Iron Eyes was unafraid.

He knew one day death would claim his sorrowful carcass, but even the Grim Reaper would have to fight mighty hard to get the better of him.

Iron Eyes crossed the wide street and headed towards a small quiet café. Its aromatic scent drew him like a bullet to a magnet. His eyes darted from behind the strands of long limp hair which veiled his face. If further trouble came seeking him, he was ready. He was always ready.

Iron Eyes stepped up on to the boardwalk outside the café and knew that he had survived on whiskey and cigars for three days of constant riding. It was now time to eat.

He entered the café.

His narrowed eyes surveyed the street coldly. He dragged a hardback chair away from a table and sat down close to the window. If there were any more hired guns in Cheyenne Falls the bounty hunter would greet them with a full belly.

'Steak,' he told the cook.

Iron Eyes placed his Navy Colts on the table before him.

He would greet them with a full belly and bullets.

5

A million stars sparkled like precious diamonds upon black velvet; they cast their eerie illumination across the desert trail and the vehicle jogging along at its slow pace towards the outskirts of the remote settlement. The sound of a bullwhip cracking alerted the townsfolk to its imminent arrival.

The battle-scarred stagecoach rocked on its springs as its massive wheels rolled over the ground. Yet this was unlike any other stagecoach. It was no longer the property of the Overland Stagecoach company, but belonged to its tiny young driver. Its scarred fabric had the mark of death upon its splintered shell as it steered out of the darkness and into the illuminated streets of Coleman City.

Lantern light cascaded from every

building along its busy main thorough-
fare and highlighted the lathered up
team and bullet-riddled coach they
towed. The sound of the livery chains
which connected its six-horse team to
its traces rang out in the streets of the
well-constructed town as the small
female sat upon the vehicle's driver's
box and guided her team down the long
street. She pushed her naked foot hard
against the brake pole and pulled back
on the long leathers.

The horses cantered to a halt. Steam
rose up into the star-filled heavens off
the backs of the six horses. Squirrel
Sally sucked on the stem of her corncob
pipe even though the tobacco had
ceased burning hours earlier. Fifty
miles of trail dust covered her nubile
form as she studied the unfamiliar town
and its inhabitants.

Clumps of dust fell from her with
every movement. She tossed her long
golden curls from her face and rested as
she observed every aspect of her
surroundings carefully. Sally rubbed the

palms of her small hands down her shirt front and then looped the reins around the brake pole before securing them.

'Well, if this ain't a real outhouse of a town,' she muttered critically.

Her keen eyes then spotted a couple of men sporting wide-brimmed Stetsons as they drunkenly staggered along the boardwalk towards her. They paused below her high perch and stared up at the tiny female lustfully. No amount of dust could hide her obvious charms from their bloodshot eyes.

'What you looking for, darling?' one of them asked in a mocking tone.

Squirrel Sally did not answer.

'I reckon if we dipped her in a trough she might be quite a looker,' the other drunkard added before steadying himself against a lantern post.

'You're right. All she needs is a wash.'

Angrily, Sally looked down at the two stationary men as one of them rested his hands upon her stagecoach. She blew dust from her face and then smiled down at the man. If the man had been sober he might have realized the danger in her sweet smile.

'Where the hell am I?' she enquired.

The tallest of the pair placed a boot upon the wheel and began to rise up the body of the vehicle. He was grinning from ear to ear as he closed in on the petite Sally.

'This happens to be Coleman City, sweetie,' he said as one of his hands reached over the edge of the driver's seat. 'What are you looking for?'

There was no expression in her face as she looked at him and gave out a meek sigh.

'I'm looking for a man,' Sally said innocently.

Both men chuckled as they grinned to one another.

'This must be your lucky day.' The more industrious of the pair had managed to throw his leg over the wooden box and was about to clamber the last few inches on to the seat when he heard the distinctive sound of a

Winchester being cocked beside him.

His eyes widened and he froze. He was straddled across the driver's seat, but not quite upon it. He was balanced precariously.

'What was that?' he asked nervously. 'What you got there, little girl?'

His question was answered when he felt the long metal barrel of the rifle being thrust into his groin. He stared at the rifle and then up into Squirrel Sally's innocent-looking face. She was not smiling as her hands pushed the rifle deeper into the most vulnerable part of his anatomy.

'Give me a real good reason why I shouldn't blow your pecker clean off, sweetheart.' She sighed as her eyelashes fluttered.

'Easy, gal,' he croaked. 'Let's not be hasty.'

She tilted the barrel upward an inch. 'But I like being hasty, friend. I like nothing better than shooting at things and you've got something stirring in them pants that I figure I oughta kill.'

The man looked down at the gleaming rifle barrel. He was engulfed by horror. Words refused to form in his mouth.

His friend looked up from the boardwalk curiously at his suddenly stationary pal. 'What did she say, Luke?'

Sally pushed the rifle barrel even harder into his pants as her small index finger stroked the trigger. 'Answer your friend, Luke,' she whispered. 'Tell him the little gal has a rifle aimed at your brains.'

Luke's face was ashen. 'I didn't mean no harm.'

'I do,' Sally said bluntly. 'I ain't shot anybody in over a week and I'm kinda tetchy.'

'Please don't shoot me,' Luke begged.

Sally lowered her head and stared through her flowing mane of curls at the terrified man. 'I told you that I'm looking for a man. My man. My betrothed. Have you seen him?'

Luke felt her slide the barrel of her

rifle across his crotch. Sweat poured down from his hatband as he tried to maintain his balance.

'What's the name of your betrothed?' he asked.

'Iron Eyes,' Sally said.

There was a different look of fear in Luke's face now. Even the lantern light which cascaded across the stagecoach could not hide it from her knowing eyes. He had heard the name of the notorious bounty hunter many times before and it chilled him to the bone.

'You're betrothed to Iron Eyes?' Luke stammered.

'Damn right.' Sally gave a sharp nod of her head and tilted the rifle barrel until his eyes crossed. 'Is he in this damn town?'

Luke shook his head. 'If he is, I ain't seen him.'

'Are you sure?' Sally asked.

'Dead sure,' Luke stammered.

She knew that nobody as scared as he was could lie when he had a rifle buried in his crotch. Her mouth twisted as her teeth gripped the stem of her corncob.

Squirrel Sally pulled her rifle back and then violently jabbed it into his groin. He yelped as every drop of air escaped his terrified soul. Then he watched her raise the rifle to her shoulder. Mustering every scrap of his energy Luke scrambled down from the stagecoach and then buckled in agony beside his friend.

'What the hell's wrong with you, Luke?' his pal asked.

Luke rested a hand on his friend. 'Don't ever let me climb up no stagecoaches again. You hear me?'

Sally stared down at the pathetic duo.

'Get going,' she shouted and then squeezed the rifle's trigger. The deafening flash sent a bullet between Luke's boots, kicking sawdust up into their faces.

She watched the two drunken men run as best they could down the street and then jerked the hand guard violently, sending a spent casing flying over her shoulder. She pulled the pipe from her lips, spat at the street and then leaned down in the box and hauled a whiskey bottle up from its dark depths.

A confused expression filled her dust-caked beauty. For the umpteenth time she had followed the mysterious Iron Eyes into an unknown land. She wondered why the bounty hunter always rode away from her without telling her where he was destined. It seemed that he was more willing to face the deadly guns of wanted outlaws rather than remain with her. It made no sense to her young, loving heart.

'Where in tarnation is that long-legged scarecrow?' Sally asked herself as she pulled the whiskey bottle's cork and took a swig of the powerful rye. She felt the warmth of the hard liquor as it burned a trail through her dust-filled throat in search of her innards. 'I oughta shoot him. That'd slow the varmint down a tad.'

Her frustration was only tempered when she heard the sound of footsteps approaching from the same direction that Luke and his pal had departed. Her eyes narrowed as she assumed the two drunken men had returned for more humiliation.

If that was what they wanted, she was more than willing to dish it out.

Faster than most men could blink she lowered the bottle and grabbed her Winchester again. She leaned from the high driver's seat and aimed the rifle at the approaching walker.

He stopped in his tracks.

Sally was about to shout out a warning when she saw the tin star gleaming in the lantern light. She lifted and aimed the rifle at the sky. Sally shook her head as her eyes peered through the amber light.

'Keep on coming, Sheriff,' Sally called out. 'I ain't gonna hurt you.'

Cautiously the lawman continued on towards the tiny female perched on top of the stagecoach. He strode towards the vehicle, paused and looked at the dishevelled young female.

'So you're the one shooting up my

quiet little town, are you?' He frowned and pushed the brim of his hat off his furrowed brow. 'I ought to tan your hide, young lady.'

The pipe fell from Squirrel Sally's mouth.

'You wouldn't dare,' she said.

Sheriff Cable Holt smiled at her. 'It sure would be fun for an old codger like me to try, though.'

'That tin star can't protect you against this,' Sally said as she patted the Winchester.

Holt looked outraged. 'Who the hell do you think you are, little girl?'

'I'm Sally Cooke,' she yelled down at the lawman.

Sheriff Holt's expression suddenly altered as he recognized her name. His head tilted as he stared at her.

'I've heard that name before someplace,' he muttered. 'But I can't recall where or when.'

She rolled her eyes and shook her head.

'My man calls me Squirrel.' Sally

rocked her head proudly.

Sheriff Holt moved closer to the stagecoach. 'And who in tarnation is your man exactly, missy?'

Squirrel Sally smiled sweetly at the lawman.

'Iron Eyes,' she purred.

Holt felt every ounce of colour drain from his face. He swallowed hard and then looked around the lantern-lit street.

'He ain't here, is he?'

Sally plucked her whiskey bottle off the driver's board and took a long swig. She sighed heavily and then shook her head in frustration.

'If he was you'd know it, old man.'

6

The streets of Cheyenne Falls grew darker and more dangerous with every passing moment. Iron Eyes had barely touched his meal even though he had spent nearly an hour pondering it. Yet the little he had consumed was enough to sustain the gaunt creature as he tossed a few coins on the table and rose back up to his daunting height. His eyes had never left the street which faced him through the small glass window-panes. He was like the animals he once hunted. He knew that at any moment the bullets of his enemies might come seeking him from the growing shadows.

His bony hands reached down to either side of the plate and picked up his Navy Colts before sliding them behind his belt buckle. He turned and moved the short distance to the door. Each step was punctuated by his large bloodstained spurs.

The evening air was much cooler than the interior of the café yet Iron Eyes did not notice. There were far more pressing things on his mind. Surviving until sunup was only one of them.

For the first time he was wasting bullets on men who did not have bounty on their heads, but were intent on his destruction.

Iron Eyes was troubled.

He pulled the door shut behind his pitifully lean frame and studied the street carefully. The saloons were as busy as any other night and yet there were few people on the streets.

It was as though they feared encountering the tall bounty hunter in case he was the monster so many tall tales had made him out to be. He moved to a wooden porch upright as the light within the café was extinguished. He heard the cook secure the café door with bolts as his skeletal fingers withdrew a long thin cigar from his deep pocket and placed it between his teeth.

Now bathed in darkness the bounty hunter was confident that the shadows would blunt any attempt by a gunman to get him in his sights.

His eyes darted around the street. If any more assassins were hiding out there in the scores of shadows, he could not see them.

Yet he was well aware that you seldom see the man who kills you. Only Big Dan had been bold enough to face him. After Iron Eyes had dispatched him to the undertaker he knew that any others would not be quite so daring. They would shoot from the darkest corners of the town rather than face him.

Iron Eyes knew there was only one sure way to find out if Corrigan's hired guns were out there watching him.

He raised his left hand and scratched his thumbnail across the top of a match. The flame flickered as he sucked smoke and filled his lungs.

He tossed the match at the sand.

There had been no shots. He chewed on the tobacco as smoke drifted through his razor-sharp teeth. Nobody was watching him, he concluded. The light of the match would have given even the worst of assassins the opportunity to get their chosen target in their gunsights.

He stepped down upon the sand and began to walk defiantly down the middle of Cheyenne Falls Main street. Bathed in the light of lanterns, Iron Eyes was an awesome sight.

A slight breeze lifted his long hair until it beat upon his wide shoulders like ghostly horses' hoofs.

The rhythmic sound continued until the bounty hunter reached one of the street's many saloons. He stepped up on to the boardwalk and leaned over its swing doors. The War Bonnet was virtually identical to the Lucky Lizard apart from the fact that it sported an upper floor. Iron Eyes placed his scrawny left hand upon the top of the swing doors and surveyed the saloon.

There were a dozen men within the barroom. Three well-tutored bargirls milled between them like fish swimming around, looking for a free drink or the possibility of something more profitable.

Iron Eyes pushed the doors inwards and entered. He then stood like a statue and silently defied anyone to leave the saloon.

Men lowered their cards and drinks and stared at him. The females knew that this strange apparition was fresh meat, but none of them had any appetite for this particular customer.

His brutalized looks showed signs from every battle he had survived over the years. The bargirls and customers somehow saw their own deaths predicted in his haunting eyes.

As the doors finally stopped rocking on their hinges, Iron Eyes began to walk. The standing men parted and allowed him to reach the bar without hindrance. The bargirls forgot years of training and also shied away from the tall bounty hunter. Smoke lingered over his macabre form as his teeth gripped the long cigar.

Iron Eyes reached the bar and turned to face the room full of eyes burning into him. He leaned back against the bar counter, rested his elbows upon it and glared through the strands of limp hair which hung down before his face.

'Listen up,' he shouted at them. 'I wanna know how many other hired guns Joe Corrigan left in Cheyenne Falls. I've had to kill me two of them so far and I'm getting mighty sore waiting for another of their yella breed to try his luck. So how many men did Corrigan hire?'

It seemed to be a futile exercise asking anyone in Cheyenne Falls anything concerning Corrigan, Iron Eyes reasoned. If they knew anything they seemed to be unwilling to share their knowledge.

It was a silence which the bounty hunter recognized only too well. He had met it many times in the past.

His deadly eyes flashed from one face to another.

'Reckon you're all scared witless,' Iron Eyes said through cigar smoke. 'Either that or you're just dumb.'

Iron Eyes shook his head and pushed himself away from the bar. He began to walk slowly back towards the swing doors when he heard an aged voice in a corner. It mumbled and the bounty hunter could not understand what it had said.

The bounty hunter paused and looked at the old man seated behind a card table. He had a bushy white beard and looked as though he did not have enough money to purchase a drink. He moved to the table and towered over the frail figure.

'What did you say, old-timer?' Iron Eyes asked through cigar smoke. 'I didn't catch it.'

The watery eyes looked at the gruesome figure.

'Corrigan paid five men to kill you

when you arrived here, boy,' the bearded man said as he stared at the green baize. 'I heard tell he offered the one who kills you a hundred-dollar bonus.'

The information fitted the theory the bounty hunter had been considering for the last few hours. Iron Eyes moved closer to the only person within the War Bonnet who did not seem to be afraid of either Corrigan or himself. He was impressed by the frail remnant of a man.

'Five men?' he queried.

The old man nodded. 'Yep, five dirty back-shooters, son. All paid to kill you. Every one of them is trying to earn that bonus the easy way. They're willing to do so because they value money more than anything else.'

Iron Eyes raised his scarred eyebrow. 'I've killed a couple of the bastards, but you reckon there are three more in Cheyenne Falls waiting to get the drop on me. Are you sure?'

The watery eyes glanced up briefly.

'Yep, I'm dead sure.'

Iron Eyes looked towards the others in the saloon. None of them had dared to warn him of the other hired killers. He returned his attention to the weathered old man and then dipped his fingers into his pocket and pulled out a golden coin. He placed it upon the palm of the wrinkled old hand gratefully.

'Much obliged,' he said.

The old man closed his hand around the gold coin and pulled it to his chest. He did not speak as he watched the gaunt figure swiftly leave the saloon leaving only a trail of cigar smoke in his wake.

One of the bargirls rushed to the old man. She sat down next to him and shook her head in disbelief at what he had just done. Her powdered face was etched with concern.

'Are you loco, Charlie?' she asked the old man. 'If any of Joe Corrigan's boys hear about you warning Iron Eyes they'll kill you as well.'

'So what?' He smiled.

'Ain't you scared?'

The old man shrugged.

'When you're as old as I am death don't scare you any more, gal,' he said. 'In fact it might even be a blessing in disguise.'

7

With her trusty Winchester cradled
under her arm, Squirrel Sally strolled
away from the livery stable where she
had paid for her team to be watered
and grained whilst she took a look
around Coleman City before continu-
ing her vain hunt for the elusive Iron
Eyes. Yet no matter how hard she
searched nobody admitted to having
seen him. Sally was tired as she
rounded a corner and began to retrace
her small footsteps back towards the
livery stable and her stagecoach.

But as she paced along the winding
street she knew only too well that
even though she could not find her
'betrothed' that did not mean he was
not in Coleman City.

The infamous bounty hunter was
only seen when he wanted to be seen.
He was a hunter like herself and

hunters were skilled at avoiding detection from prying eyes. That was how they crept up on their unsuspecting prey.

Sally balanced the deadly rifle on her slender shoulder and continued to study every saloon as she wearily made her way back to her stagecoach. The town was busy and yet few gave the dust-caked little female a second look. None of the citizens of Coleman City suspected that anyone so small could be as dangerous as she was.

Sheriff Cable Holt wandered out on to the street just as Sally came into view. The veteran lawman felt his chest tighten as he stared at her perfect form wandering straight towards him. He turned on his heels and rushed into a dark alley and then crouched behind a large water barrel and waited for her to pass.

Sally kicked at the sand beneath her feet as she approached the telegraph office. She yawned and pulled the Winchester off her shoulder and placed it down against a water trough outside the building. She sat on the edge of the water trough and rubbed her bare feet vigorously.

'Damn you, Iron Eyes.' She cursed under her breath. 'When I get my hands on you I'll string you up by your thumbs, you long-legged bastard.'

Sally pulled a twisted cigar from her shirt pocket and placed it between her lips. As she struck a match and raised it towards the cigar, she could hear the constant tapping of the telegraph key inside the office.

Then another far louder noise drew her attention. It was two horses thundering towards her. Her beautiful eyes narrowed as she focused on two horsemen spurring their mounts from out of the darkness.

'Cowboys.' She sighed. 'I hate cowboys.'

Remaining exactly where she was, Sally inhaled the acrid smoke and continued to sit defiantly on the trough as they drew closer.

She had learned long ago never to show fear.

As smoke filtered from her lips, the riders hauled rein only yards from her. Sally watched as one of them leapt from his saddle as his pal controlled both their mounts.

The cowboy jumped over the trough, mounted the boardwalk and entered the telegraph office hurriedly. It seemed strange to her that anyone could be so eager to either send or collect a telegraph message. She turned on the trough and lowered her aching feet into the water to soothe them.

From the corner of her eye she could see the mounted cowboy looking down at her. She glanced through her wavy curls at him as he leaned on his saddle horn and smiled at her.

He touched his hat brim. 'Howdy, ma'am.'

Sally pulled the cigar from her lips and frowned at him.

'Howdy yourself,' she said before poking her tongue at the cowboy. 'I'm spoken for. I'm practically married.'

The horseman shrugged. 'You are?'

Sally grabbed her Winchester.

'What you mean by that?' she pouted.

The horseman did not have time to reply. The door of the telegraph office opened again. Lantern light washed over the street and Sally watched the more athletic of the cowboys emerge and run back to his horse. He had a slip of paper in his hand and was waving it as he mounted.

'What you got there?' the other cowboy asked.

'This is a wire for Drako Sharp,' came the reply. 'I gotta deliver it. There's a silver dollar in it for me.'

'Drako Sharp, the gunfighter?'

The cowboy nodded as he tugged on his leathers and turned his mount. 'Yep, he got a place on the outskirts of town. I've got to deliver this wire to him pronto. Some hombre named Bevis in Cheyenne Falls wants him there.'

'What for?'

The first cowboy tucked the message into his pocket and held his reins in both hands. 'It's got something to do with a varmint named Iron Eyes. I bet Bevis wants to hire Sharp to kill this Iron Eyes critter.'

Squirrel Sally pulled the cigar from her lips as their words filled her young mind.

So Iron Eyes is in Cheyenne Falls, she thought.

Both cowboys whipped the long leathers of their reins across the tails of their horses and galloped back into the darkness.

'Somebody in Cheyenne Falls wants my Iron Eyes dead,' she mumbled as she swung her legs out of the refreshing water and placed them back on the sand. 'I gotta get to Cheyenne Falls fast and warn him.'

With her Winchester gripped firmly in her hands the young female ran as quickly as her tired legs would carry her back towards the livery stable. With each stride she thought about the conversation she had overheard.

Whoever Drako Sharp was the cowboys had called him a gunfighter. As she crossed the street towards the battered stagecoach another more accurate description for Sharp came to mind.

Hired gunman.

That was what Drako Sharp really was.

Sally reached the livery stable and frantically clambered up to the driver's seat of the stagecoach. She placed her trusty rifle on the driver's board and then untied the hefty reins from around the brake pole. All she could think about was her beloved Iron Eyes.

The blacksmith ran from out of the stable and stared at the feisty female. He stopped in his tracks as the deceptively sweet face looked down at him.

'Which way do I go to get to Cheyenne Falls?' Sally yelled at the muscular man. 'Which way?'

He pointed due west. 'Thataway, missy.'

'Thank you kindly,' she said as her mind returned to the man she loved. She knew that Iron Eyes could more than match anyone with his guns, but what if Drako Sharp was a back-shooter? Just the thought gave her goosebumps.

Sally released the brake and then expertly unleashed her bullwhip. The long, woven leather cracked like a thunderbolt above the team of horses. The team dug their hoofs into the sand and pulled their heavy burden away from the livery.

A cloud of dust billowed up into the night air as the six horses responded to the cracking bullwhip. Within a heart-beat they were thundering in the direction of Cheyenne Falls.

As the blacksmith scratched his bald head Sheriff Holt appeared from the shadows and stood beside the strong figure watching the departing stage-coach as it sped out of town at breakneck speed.

'Thank the Lord she's gone,' Holt

said as he mopped his brow. 'We don't need females in this town who belong to Iron Eyes.'

The blacksmith glanced at the lawman. 'You know something, Sheriff? That little gal scared the life out of me.'

Sheriff Holt licked his dry lips. 'I believe you.'

8

The night air whistled along the streets of Cheyenne Falls; it sounded like a freight train approaching. Yet it was only the haunting noise of the desert sand as it tormented and confused the weary as they made their way from saloon to saloon. Within the confines of the remote desert town there were three men who neither noticed nor cared about the weird sounds from the surrounding dunes. The hired killers made their way closer to the heart of the settlement from various corners of the town.

Not even rats could have used the shadows to their advantage quite as well as the heavily armed gunmen. They scurried like vermin towards their meeting place. Cheyenne Falls was quiet for the moment, but soon it would once again resound with the deafening noise that only six-shooters could produce.

They had death on their minds as they closed in on the tall livery stable. The three remaining gunmen whom Joe Corrigan had hired moved unseen towards the gloomy stables. Each came from a different direction to gather in the one place they considered safe.

They knew that the stableman always went for his supper at this time of night leaving the huge building empty apart from the horses which were stalled beneath its vaulted roof. The glowing of coals in the forge gave the interior of the building a scarlet hue as Bob Lane, Ralph Wood and Davy Cooper entered.

The gunmen gathered beside the warm forge.

Cooper checked his guns were fully loaded as his cohorts sat down beside the blaze. The gang had killed many men for Joe Corrigan in order to prevent any bounty hunters from trailing him as the outlaw travelled on to Devil's Canyon.

Yet this time was different from all the previous occasions when they had mindlessly taken their blood money. This time their numbers had been reduced by two.

Iron Eyes was no ordinary bounty hunter as Joe Corrigan had led them to believe. He was as deadly as the men he hunted if not deadlier. Few men had ever survived an encounter with the gaunt, emaciated Iron Eyes. Even to try was regarded as suicidal.

Cooper knew that his last two remaining allies were scared, but he had a plan. One which he felt would end the life of the notorious bounty hunter.

'We gotta get this right, boys,' Cooper said as he warmed his hands over the glowing coals. 'Big Dan and Steve underestimated that bounty hunter and I don't want to end up like them.'

'Iron Eyes ain't like any of the others.' Lane brooded.

Cooper nodded. 'He sure is mighty handy with them guns of his. I've never seen anyone as accurate as he is.'

Wood nodded. 'I've heard tell that Iron Eyes is called the living ghost by Injuns.'

Lane rubbed his jaw thoughtfully. 'Yeah, they say that he can't be killed 'coz he's already dead. Corrigan never told us that it was Iron Eyes we had to kill.'

Cooper straightened up and rested his hands on the grips of his guns. He shook his head and laughed.

'Believe me, Iron Eyes is alive OK,' he said firmly. 'And anything alive can be killed. Big Dan and Steve just went about it all wrong.'

Lane and Wood were not so confident.

'Joe didn't tell us that Iron Eyes was the bounty hunter we were meant to bushwhack, Davy.' Wood shrugged. 'I'd not have taken his money if I'd known that.'

'If Joe had been straight with us Dan and Steve might still be alive,' Lane added fretfully. 'Iron Eyes just ain't like other varmints. That bastard is in league with the Devil himself.'

Davy Cooper grabbed the collars of both men and hauled them to their feet. His head pressed between them. 'Listen up and quit snivelling, boys. We're gonna kill him just like Joe paid us to do. Iron Eyes has just been lucky. But luck can run sour.'

They both looked at Cooper.

'But how are we gonna kill him?' Wood moaned. 'Steve and Big Dan sure failed.'

'Yeah, Davy,' Lane said. 'How are we gonna do better? Iron Eyes is quicksilver. We can't outdraw him.'

Cooper released his grip on his cohorts and strolled to the large wooden doors. He was totally confident, unlike the others. His eyes narrowed as they stared along the street at the hotel veranda. He raised his hand and pointed at the window of Iron Eyes's room.

'What you looking at, Davy,' Lane asked as he and Woods walked to the stable entrance.

'The hotel room,' Cooper replied. 'I followed him there when he left the War Bonnet.'

Woods and Lane moved to either side of their thoughtful comrade.

'I reckon Iron Eyes is up in there right now getting himself some shut-eye before he sets out after Joe in the morning,' Cooper reasoned. 'Steve made a mistake and went to that room on his lonesome. He might have run, but not fast enough. All we gotta do is work together. We gotta strike together as a team. Even Iron Eyes can't fend off bullets that are coming at him from different directions. We fill that room with hot lead from the room door and the window at exactly the same time. Iron Eyes can't defend his sorrowful hide against a sustained attack.'

Lane smiled. 'That's right. If we empty every bullet in our guns at him he's gotta die. There ain't no way he can survive.'

'Now you're talking sense, Bob.' Cooper rested his hands on his gun grips and continued to eye the hotel. 'We have two guns each. Even the infamous Iron Eyes can't avoid three dozen bullets when they're fired at him.'

'We can't miss.' Wood rubbed his hands together.

'How we gonna do it, Davy?' Lane asked.

Cooper glanced at his cohorts. 'You boys will go down the alley and enter the hotel by the side door. That way Bevis or that dumb nephew of his won't see you when you use the back stairs. At the same time I'll head on up to the veranda and go to his window. When I start shooting through the window you boys will kick the door in and start firing. I reckon he'll be asleep when he meets his Maker.'

'Dead asleep.' Lane grinned.

They checked that their weaponry was fully loaded just as Cooper had done a few moments earlier.

'When do we do it?' Wood asked eagerly.

Cooper glanced at them. 'Right now! C'mon, boys. Let's go kill a ghost.'

The three gunmen left the livery stable, fanned out and headed towards the hotel. Yet even though they were convinced that Iron Eyes was asleep in his hotel room the trio of hired killers were still cautious of being observed. They moved in the shadows stealthily towards their goal like the vermin they truly were.

Beneath the canopy of glittering stars Lane and Wood did exactly as instructed and headed down the dark alley beside the hotel towards the side door set at the very end of the building. Cooper followed a few steps behind them to the wooden steps and then started up towards the veranda.

When he reached the veranda, Cooper paused and watched as his two fellow gunmen entered the side door into the hotel. After giving Lane and Wood enough time to reach the corridor he began to walk slowly towards the window.

The strange sound of the desert breeze filled Cooper's ears as the deadly killer rested his back against the wooden wall. He cautiously peered into the room. The lace drapes fluttered like the wings of a butterfly, indicating that the window was not quite shut.

He reached down and forced his fingers into the gap. He then opened the sash window. Cooper's eyes squinted into the unlit room at the bed.

His well-trained hands drew both his guns.

Davy Cooper began to fire his weapons. The room lit up as deafening flashes of lethal lead spewed from his gun barrels and tore into the bed. He had barely fired his .45s twice when he saw the room door kicked open and his fellow hired killers blasting their own guns into the bed.

The acrid stench of gunsmoke filled the room as all three of the gunmen emptied the last of their bullets into what was left of the bed. The smoke hung on the air and burned their eyes as they tried to see the dead body in the bed.

Lane raced forward and tore the bullet-riddled sheets from the bed. To his surprise he saw nothing but more smouldering bullet holes.

There was no body.

No Iron Eyes.

'He ain't here.' Lane gasped as Wood ran to his side and tore every sheet off the bed.

'He ain't here, Davy,' Wood shouted at his pal on the veranda. 'Iron Eyes ain't here. Where is he?'

Lane was shaking as he turned to Wood.

'You can't kill something that's already dead.'

'Maybe them tall stories ain't as tall after all.'

Cooper heard the words of his terrified cohorts and felt the cold rush of panic tear through his body as well. He holstered one gun and then shook the spent casings from the other.

'Reload them guns as fast as you can,

boys,' Cooper yelled at the top of his voice. 'Iron Eyes has tricked us. Quick. Get down to the alley. I'll meet you there.'

Then as his fingers desperately fumbled with bullets from his gun belt Cooper heard another sound. A far more spine-chilling sound. It was not the ghostly noise the desert sand made but an even stranger one, he thought.

But what was it?

Cooper moved to the veranda railing and stared down into the amber lantern light. He did not know it, but soon his question would be answered.

9

The strange buzzing sound grew louder as the thin figure of Iron Eyes moved out of the shadows opposite the hotel with a cutting rope in his hands. He had the rope spinning above his head at such a speed that it sounded like a swarm of angry hornets. Iron Eyes had waited until he was positive that the hired gunman on the veranda had emptied every bullet from his guns. Then he started to advance across the street with the spinning loop of his cutting rope above his head. His narrowed eyes stared up at the confused Davy Cooper, who was leaning over the veranda.

A pool of orange light cascaded over the bounty hunter as he stepped into it. The answer Cooper had been seeking suddenly appeared.

Cooper felt his heart quicken at the

hideous sight. It was like looking into the bowels of hell. Iron Eyes kept walking towards the hotel with the rope held in his bony hand spinning faster and faster above his head.

The gunman's eyes widened in terror.

'Iron Eyes,' he gasped.

The words had only just crept from his lips when he saw the pitifully thin bounty hunter release the twirling lasso and propel it up at him. The rope wriggled through the desert air like a sidewinder.

Frantically Cooper went to fire and then realized that he had not finished reloading his six-shooter. As his hands attempted to close the partially loaded chamber of the weapon he felt the large circle of rope surround him.

Seeing that his aim was true Iron Eyes leaned back and tugged on the rope as it fell over Cooper's torso. The lasso tightened as the bounty hunter gave one mighty pull on its taut length.

The lasso had wrapped around the

gunman's arms and chest.

Iron Eyes gritted his teeth and mustered every ounce of his strength. He gave a massive tug.

Cooper screamed and was lifted off his feet. He flew helplessly over the railing and then fell like a stone from his high perch.

Iron Eyes released his hold on the rope as Cooper hit the ground head first. A cloud of dust rose up from where the gunman had crashed into the sand.

Even before the skeletal figure began to run to the prostrate body he knew that the gunman was dead.

He had heard Cooper's neck snap as it had impacted into the unforgiving street. The bounty hunter reached the body and stared down upon it.

Iron Eyes knelt and stared at the dead man just as Lane and Wood came rushing out of the alley twenty feet away from the bloodstained sand. Both of Cooper's cohorts stopped in their tracks and stared in horror at the scarred face of the kneeling bounty hunter.

The flickering light from untold numbers of lanterns cast their eerie illumination across his hideous features as Iron Eyes glared at the other two hired killers. He was like a ravenous wolf suddenly faced by innocent lambs.

Even the Devil himself could not have appeared more terrifying to Lane and Wood as they stared in disbelief at the creature bent over Cooper's corpse. It was as if every one of their previous victim's ghosts had suddenly manifested into a drooling monster. Iron Eyes glared through his long, limp hair at them. Both the hired guns realized that this was not a man like any other man. He would make them pay for all their past sins.

'Kill him,' Lane screamed out.

'That's just what I aim to do.' Ralph Wood cocked his reloaded Colt and blasted it at the kneeling Iron Eyes. He watched in shock as his bullet tore through the bounty hunter's raised collar. His shaking hand cocked the gun again as Iron Eyes slowly rose up from Cooper's body.

Wood fired again.

This time his bullet kicked up a cloud of sand just beyond the broken body of Cooper. Iron Eyes rose up to his full height.

Wood turned and looked for Lane, but it was a futile exercise. Bob Lane had already run back into the alley and would not stop running until he found a horse.

'You yella bastard, Bob,' Wood snarled before returning his gaze to the silent Iron Eyes. It was like facing the Devil in human form.

Ralph Wood was the perfect picture of absolute terror as he backed away from the awesome bounty hunter. Sweat ran down his face as he watched Iron Eyes pull one of his Navy Colts from his belt.

Wood swallowed hard, cocked his gun again and went to aim the smoking weapon at the frightening sight. The bounty hunter swiftly cocked and fired his Navy Colt.

His aim was straight and true.

The coal-tar lantern which hung from the hotel porch illuminated the plume of scarlet droplets which burst from Wood's chest as he flew backwards and landed on a hitching pole. The pole snapped in half as the gunman crashed through its weathered length.

Another sound of snapping filled the bounty hunter's ears as he approached the body. Iron Eyes stared down at the dead man and knew that it had not just been the pole which had broken.

The way Wood lay on the ground told Iron Eyes that the hired killer's back had also broken as he had hit the hitching rail.

There was no sign of emotion in the face of the bounty hunter as he listened to the sound of a horse galloping away from Cheyenne Falls.

Bob Lane was riding hard. The gunman was putting distance between himself and the fearsome bounty hunter. Iron Eyes turned and started to walk towards the livery stable.

He was halfway there when he saw the glinting tin star of Sheriff Cord as the lawman cut in front of him. Iron Eyes did not pause, but continued to stride towards the livery stable.

'They started it, Sheriff,' he drawled.

'I know that.'

The long-legged bounty hunter glanced over his shoulder at the lawman, who was attempting to match his stride.

'Then what the hell do you want?'

'Where you going, Iron Eyes?' Cord asked as he tried to keep pace with the far longer legs.

'I'm going after Joe Corrigan, Sheriff,' Iron Eyes answered as he entered the livery stable and marched up to his palomino stallion.

'You're headed to Devil's Canyon?' Cord said as he watched the thin bounty hunter lead his magnificent horse from its stall and start to saddle it.

'Is that where that yella back-shooter

is headed?' Iron Eyes asked as he patted the blanket down on the back of his mount.

Josiah Cord nodded. 'He was headed that way. I'd say that he's going to tell Corrigan that him and his cronies failed to kill you.'

Iron Eyes lifted the hefty Mexican saddle and threw it on top of the blanket. He reached under the belly of the stallion and pulled the cinch strap towards him.

'Good. All I gotta do is follow the coward's hoof tracks and he'll lead me straight to Corrigan,' he said as he threaded the cinch strap through a metal ring and tightened it. 'Then I'll kill them.'

Sheriff Cord edged closer to the far taller man. 'It ain't as easy as you seem to think, boy. As far as I know most of the folks that head into Devil's Canyon don't ever return.'

Iron Eyes secured the strap and lowered the fender. He looked down into the face of the troubled lawman.

'What's eating at you?' he asked.

'You ain't listening. Devil's Canyon is plumb dangerous, Iron Eyes,' Sheriff Cord insisted. 'It's full of caves the Cheyenne dug years back. Dozens of varmints have died in them. Joe Corrigan is the only critter who ain't fallen foul of them damn caves.'

'So?'

'I'm just trying to warn you, son.' Cord shrugged.

Iron Eyes stepped into his stirrup and lifted his lean frame up on to the elegant saddle. He gathered up his reins and turned the powerful stallion.

'You've warned me. I'm obliged,' Iron Eyes said. 'But I don't intend dying like all them other critters you've told me about, Sheriff. I intend killing.'

Sheriff Cord followed the stallion as it walked out into the lantern-lit street. He shook his head.

'Corrigan might be an outlaw but he's got plenty of friends in Cheyenne Falls, boy. They'll do anything to help that varmint,' the lawman warned.

'You've seen their loyalty at first hand.'

Iron Eyes looked thoughtful. 'Corrigan buys his brand of loyalty, Sheriff. It ain't worth a plug nickel when the chips are down.'

'I hope you're right, Iron Eyes,' Cord said. 'I wish you luck anyway.'

Iron Eyes patted the gun grips which poked out from behind his belt buckle. He leaned down from his saddle and whispered into the sheriff's ear.

'I don't need luck, I've got these beauties, Sheriff,' Iron Eyes explained. 'Unlike most of the folks that I've met over the years, they've never let me down.'

Josiah Cord inhaled and watched as the bounty hunter swung his mount around and then rammed his spurs deep into the stallion's flesh.

The high-shouldered horse reared up and then as its hoofs touched the sand once more it thundered away from the livery stable and headed towards the desert. The sight of the determined horseman sent chills down the spine of the weathered sheriff.

The lawman exhaled and watched as Iron Eyes stood in his stirrups and urged the powerful palomino on. Cord rubbed his whiskered face and wondered how long anyone like the bounty hunter could continue his relentless quest. When would Lady Luck finally shy away from the scarred creature she had protected for so long?

'There's always a first time, Iron Eyes,' he muttered.

10

Devil's Canyon was, just as its name implied, an unholy place set in an ocean of sand. The canyon walls were honeycombed with countless caves. Most were natural whilst others had been carved out of the rocks by men in search of the golden ore rumoured to be within one of their dark confines. Legend said that the once mighty Cheyenne had discovered a rich vein of the precious element in one of the caves and fashioned beautiful ornaments from it. That was long before the white man had driven them out of their homelands and vainly attempted to find out which of the caves held the secret fortune.

Few men had survived the extreme temperatures found in the desert, unless they were well prepared. Even fewer had wasted a fortune needed in the search for the elusive vein of gold. Yet that was exactly what the deadly outlaw Joe Corrigan had done. He had become totally obsessed by the prospect of being the first man since the Cheyenne to discover it.

The bank robber had once found a gold nugget near the mouth of one of its many caves and over the years he had returned over and over again in his search for the mother-load he believed was waiting to be discovered. Yet apart from the occasional small handful of nuggets he had failed.

Corrigan had become yet another victim of gold fever.

Unlike the many previous gold rushes which had seen thousands of normal hard-working men abandon their families and risk everything in search of finding their own fortunes, few men had ever survived long enough to even reach the remote outcrop of rocks. The desert had culled most who had vainly attempted to find Devil's Canyon.

A mere handful of men knew how to get to and from the deadly caves safely. Corrigan and his most trusted hired guns were privy to the secret. Countless others had found to their cost that even if they survived the desert the guns of Corrigan would end their quest permanently.

The gold fever Corrigan suffered from had engulfed the outlaw's mind almost to the point of insanity. He rarely left the canyon and when he did venture back into the relative civilization found in various large towns it was merely to rob and kill mercilessly. When he returned from these trips, he would squander most of his loot on paying his hired gunmen to kill anyone who might be on his trail.

What was left of the money he had stolen was ploughed into the vain quest for riches. Corrigan had spent a fortune in search of another fortune.

The once elegant outlaw had become a shadow of his former self. The mania which drove him on and on searching for the legendary vein of gold had given him the look of so many other prospectors.

There was only one difference.

No other gold miner wore a hand-tooled gun belt with twin holsters and a pair of matched Remington .45s. Corrigan had spent the last few years searching one cave after another and each time he entered one of the dark tunnels his fevered mind told him that this time he would be successful.

Since his last job Corrigan had known that he was being trailed by a bounty hunter. His last bank robbery had been even more brutal than those which had gone before and when he had ridden through Cheyenne Falls on his way back to the lethal canyon he hired five men to be alert and kill the bounty hunter as soon as he entered the town.

Had Corrigan known that it was the legendary Iron Eyes who dogged his trail he might have chosen to lie in wait for his hunter to show himself, yet he had never imagined that the cold-blooded Iron Eyes would ever pick him as his next potential target.

In the past there had never been any problems about his hired guns doing what they were paid to do. On several occasions they had earned their blood money easily and killed anyone who dared to follow Corrigan. That was until they had faced the intrepid bounty hunter.

Iron Eyes had other ideas.

He was not ready to die.

Just like his men, Corrigan had underestimated the true determination of Iron Eyes. Even if he had known the outlaw might still have not been alarmed. For like so many other outlaws Corrigan imagined that most of the tall tales concerning the lethal predator were just that.

Nothing more than tall tales.

The desert night was as silent as always as Corrigan moved out from yet another cave, and dropped his pick and lantern. He rubbed the embedded grime from his hardened features and rested for a few moments to survey the rolling dunes from his high vantage point. He was about to head down to his well-equipped wagon when something drew his attention.

The outlaw's cruel eyes focused upon the distant desert sand like an eagle.

It was the cloud of hoof dust which alerted Corrigan that someone was riding fast across the rolling dunes towards the canyon of caves. He watched the rider drawing ever closer to Devil's Canyon and knew that someone was coming to join him — that only meant trouble. Even though all of his hired gunmen knew the only safe route to and from Devil's Canyon none of them had ever dared put that knowledge into practice.

Something was wrong, Corrigan realized.

The starlight danced upon the horseman as he drove his mount closer and closer. Totally confident in his ability to kill anyone who dared invade the deadly canyon, Corrigan was unconcerned until his keen eyes noticed another cloud of dust a mile or so behind the first rider.

There were two riders heading towards the canyon; both were whipping their long leathers across the tails of their mounts and approaching the canyon at breakneck pace. One seemed desperate to reach the canyon whilst the other doggedly followed.

Something was wrong.

Corrigan adjusted his gun belt and picked up his rifle. For the first time in more than a year someone had managed to survive Cheyenne Falls and continue on to Devil's Canyon.

Corrigan squinted in a bitter effort to try and make out the horsemen. Yet the strange bluish starlight made identifying them impossible.

Although it was impossible to work out who the riders were, his instincts told him that only one of his hirelings would dare approach the canyon. The second rider was a different kettle of fish altogether, though. Corrigan knew he had to be the same bounty hunter whom he had become aware of when he had returned from his last bank robbery.

Whoever he was, Corrigan surmised, he would not give up.

He scratched a match down the cave wall thoughtfully and lit his crude cigarette as his eyes remained glued to the approaching riders.

Smoke trailed Corrigan as he moved down to the floor of the canyon and rested against his provision wagon. His eyes darted to his saddle horse and the two muscular nags he used to draw the prairie schooner. They were corralled in the canyon and well away from any line of fire which he was certain would soon break out.

With his Winchester gripped firmly in his hands, Corrigan walked to his campfire, kicked sand over its flames and then ventured back to the front of the vehicle.

Like many troubled men, Corrigan

talked to himself constantly; his eyes narrowed and stared through the eerie starlight at the approaching riders.

'Damned if I know who you critters are but you've both made a mighty big mistake coming here,' Corrigan snarled. 'This is my land. You ain't stealing my thunder. I've worked too damn hard looking for that vein of gold.'

He pushed the hand guard down and expelled a spent casing from the magazine. He jerked the guard back up and curled his finger around the trigger.

'Keep on coming,' Corrigan said as he rested the barrel of the deadly carbine on the body of the wagon. 'You'll learn soon enough that it don't pay to come here. I'll surely kill you when you come into range.'

The once sane outlaw was now little more than a maniac consumed by gold fever. Every fibre of his being wanted to protect the fortune in gold he had yet to discover.

His eyes carefully watched as the horsemen steered their mounts through the dunes and continued on towards the canyon he had come to consider his property.

'Damn this starlight,' Corrigan cursed. 'Why ain't there a moon when you need one?'

The cloudless black sky was peppered with an untold number of sparkling stars. Their light cast an eerie hue across the vast expanse of desert which faced the disturbed outlaw.

It was impossible to see who it was riding towards him, but Corrigan sensed that it had to be one of the many men he had paid to kill the bounty hunter when he reached Cheyenne Falls.

Questions raced through his mind. No matter how hard he considered them, there were no answers.

Even so his finger still itched to pull back on his rifle trigger. It had been the better part of two weeks since he had last killed anyone and Corrigan was eager to satisfy his bloodthirsty desire again.

'Keep on coming, boys.' Corrigan laughed to himself. 'One of you bastards is gonna make my day and eat lead.'

He edged closer to the corner of the wagon with the rifle held in his muscular arms. He started to see the first rider in more detail as the horseman came within range of his Winchester.

He had been right, he thought. It was one of his men.

'That's Bob Lane,' Corrigan told himself before wondering, 'What's that dumb critter doing here? I told him and the rest of the boys to stay in town and kill the bounty hunter when he showed his face.'

A chill traced up the spine of the rifleman.

'Lane wouldn't have come here unless the others are dead,' Corrigan muttered as his confused mind tried to explain why one of his trusty henchmen would ignore his orders. 'There's only one bastard that could kill all of them other boys.'

Reaching the wagon, Bob Lane dragged rein and dropped on to the sand. He held on to his leathers and led his lathered-up horse up to the outlaw. Corrigan stared blankly at the terrified face.

Lane looked back through the rising dust at the rider who was doggedly following him. He pointed and stammered.

'That's Iron Eyes, Joe,' Lane managed to say.

Corrigan lowered his rifle and stared at the horseman who was still defiantly approaching.

'Iron Eyes?' He repeated the name.

'Yep.' Lane slapped the tail of his mount and sent it trotting towards the other horses. He then drew both his guns and edged closer to the stunned outlaw. 'That's Iron Eyes OK, Joe.'

A fury erupted inside Corrigan. He turned and grabbed Lane's collar. 'Where are the rest of the boys? Why ain't they here with you? Why?'

Lane pointed a gun at the intrepid rider beyond the hoof-dust cloud.

'They're all dead. He killed them, Joe,' Lane said. 'I only just escaped by the skin of my teeth while he was killing Ralph and Davy. I came to warn you.'

Corrigan pulled Lane closer. His eyes burned into the terrified gunman.

'What about Big Dan and Steve?' he growled.

Lane shook his head.

'They're dead too. Iron Eyes killed them first,' he stammered. 'That critter ain't human.'

Dust rose into the black sky above the desert from the approaching hoofs. Corrigan thought quickly and then pointed to his wagon.

'Get up in there, Bob,' he ordered with a snarl. 'I got a box of dynamite sticks and fuses in there. Get a handful of both and bring them down here. Not even Iron Eyes can survive being blown apart by dynamite.'

Lane did not need telling twice. He ran to the back of the canvased wagon, lowered its tailgate and climbed up into it in search of the explosives.

Corrigan squinted into the blinding dust which tormented his sore eyes and yet could no longer see the haunting bounty hunter. Only the sound of the powerful stallion's hoofs told the outlaw that Iron Eyes was still making fearlessly for the canyon.

Most men would have become nervous when they couldn't see the infamous bounty hunter, but not the troubled outlaw. He grew angrier that his cherished canyon was being invaded.

Corrigan sucked the last of the smoke from his cigarette as the sound of the pounding hoofs grew louder and louder with every beat of his heart.

'Keep on coming, Iron Eyes,' Corrigan shouted furiously. 'I'll teach you that it don't pay to kill my boys. Now it's your turn to die.'

He spat his cigarette at the sand and raised the rifle back up to his shoulder. The sound of the palomino stallion grew even louder. Corrigan knew that it was only a matter of seconds before Iron Eyes would ride through the dust cloud and be a target he could not miss.

Corrigan was about to fire when he saw the powerful horse burst through the blinding dust cloud. His eyes widened in disbelief.

'What the hell?' he screamed in anger.

Corrigan lowered his rifle and swallowed hard as his fevered mind tried to accept what his eyes were staring at. He staggered forward just as Lane jumped down beside him with an armful of dynamite sticks and fuses.

Lane also stared with unbelieving eyes at the magnificent palomino stallion before them. He looked at Corrigan for an explanation, but could see that the hardened outlaw was also dumbfounded.

The stallion had stopped a few yards from the barrel of the Winchester. It snorted and clawed at the sand with its hoof. Corrigan and Lane stood by the handsome animal in stunned disbelief.

Iron Eyes was no longer in the saddle.

11

Totally bewildered, Corrigan stared at the powerful palomino and its empty saddle. He swung his rifle around in search of the infamous bounty hunter, but there was no sign of Iron Eyes anywhere. It was as though he had simply vanished into thin air a fraction of a second before his mount burst through the cloud of hoof dust.

There was no sign of the deadly hunter of wanted men.

'Where the hell is he, Joe?' Lane asked desperately as he cradled the explosives in his shaking arms. 'Where did Iron Eyes disappear to?'

Corrigan had no answer. He backed away from the elegant stallion and ushered Lane back towards the canyon walls and the array of caves.

'C'mon, Bob,' he growled as he kept his rifle trained on every shadow. 'Let's get up to them caves before that varmint shows himself. We can pick him off once he shows himself.'

Both men rushed towards the starlit rocks. Corrigan allowed Lane to scale the loose gravel first whilst he covered him with his Winchester.

When Lane had scrambled over the rim of the slope and moved into one of the cave entrances Corrigan turned and raced up the slope after him. Corrigan dropped down beside his hired gunman and helped the younger man to carefully place the sticks of dynamite and fuses down between them.

Lane removed his Stetson and crouched down at the mouth of the cave. He pulled his guns from their holsters and pointed them down into the canyon yet there was no target. Wherever Iron Eyes had gone neither could see him.

Corrigan worked feverishly and rammed fuses into the sticks of deadly explosive.

'Can you see him, Bob?' Corrigan

asked as he completed his task and moved to the shoulder of the frightened man.

Lane licked his dry lips. 'All I can see is the wagon and the horses.'

'Damn it all,' Corrigan cursed. 'Nobody can just vanish into thin air. He has to be down there someplace. Keep looking, Bob. Keep looking.'

Lane nodded. 'How did he disappear like that, Joe? Like you said, it ain't possible.'

'It must be possible. He did it, didn't he?' Corrigan said as the question tormented him.

Lane eyed the outlaw, but remained silent. He was unsure whether he was more afraid of Corrigan or Iron Eyes.

Corrigan ran the short distance to the other side of the cave entrance and peered down into the haunting light. Just like Lane he was able to see the wagon and the stallion as well as his own horses, but apart from that he could not make out anything. The canyon was filled with long black shadows. They played tricks with his eyes.

'Iron Eyes must have jumped off that stallion just before it raced through your hoof dust, Bob,' Corrigan said as he checked his holstered guns carefully before cradling his rifle again.

Lane glanced across at Corrigan. 'It would take some mighty perfect timing to do that without breaking your neck, Joe.'

'If all the stories I've heard about that critter are true, Iron Eyes would risk his neck to get his hands on bounty money.' Corrigan stared down the slope to the canyon floor with his rifle in readiness. 'He's just a damn coward. He was scared to face us like a man. He intends back-shooting us both.'

'You're wrong. I saw Iron Eyes back at Cheyenne Falls, Joe,' Lane said. 'He sure ain't no coward. He faced Big Dan and the rest of us square on. That critter is the meanest man I've ever set eyes upon.'

Corrigan looked at Lane. 'How did

you manage to escape without getting shot up like the rest of the boys, Bob?'

Lane rested on one knee and shrugged.

'I ran like a yella dog, Joe,' he admitted. 'When I saw him kneeling over Cooper's body I knew we couldn't beat him to the draw. Ralph got brave, but I ran. I reckoned it was safer to come here to warn you than face him and end up as dead as the rest of the boys.'

The expression upon the face of Corrigan altered. Suddenly it went as dark as the night sky. His eyes burned into Lane angrily.

'You ran away?'

Lane nodded. 'I sure did.'

Corrigan exhaled through his flared nostrils. 'You dumb bastard. You led him here. Iron Eyes might never have found me if he hadn't been able to trail you. I thought it was funny that he didn't even try to shoot you, he was following your sorry hide.'

'I'm sorry, Joe.' Lane lowered his

head and stared at his guns. 'I didn't intend leading him to you. I was so plumb scared that I figured the safest place was here with you.'

Corrigan rubbed his sleeve across his brow.

'Reckon the damage has already bin done,' he reasoned. 'I got me a feeling that you've done me a favour really. You've led the most ruthless bounty hunter straight to where he'll die.'

Lane smiled and nodded. 'You'll kill him, Joe. You'll put an end to Iron Eyes for good. Every outlaw in the territory will be in your debt.'

'I'll kill them as well if they come here.'

Lane looked into the cave. 'Have you prospected this particular cave, Joe?'

'Nope,' Corrigan replied. 'I ain't got to this one yet.'

Suddenly he noticed something down below their vantage point moving in the shadows. He edged closer to the rim.

'Did you see that, Bob.' Corrigan pointed. 'Down there by the wagon. I saw something moving.'

'Iron Eyes?'

'It has to be.' Corrigan chuckled. 'I knew he'd break his cover sooner or later.'

Bob Lane stood and aimed his six-shooters down towards the wagon. He looked hard upon the canvased vehicle and then he too spotted movement behind it.

'I seen him as well, Joe,' Lane said excitedly. 'He's down behind the wagon OK. Should I open up on him?'

Corrigan reached across to Lane. 'No. Wait.'

'Wait?' Lane looked confused. 'But why?'

'We don't want to start shooting down at my wagon, Bob,' Corrigan explained. 'I've got my provisions in there as well as more explosives. I've also got two water barrels strapped to its sides.'

Lane lowered his guns. 'That was a close one. If I'd started shooting I might have hit them explosives and blown the wagon sky high.'

Corrigan relaxed for a moment. Then he looked anxious as he realized that they had been separated from everything they needed to survive in the desert. Their water, grub and dynamite were out of reach.

Lane looked across at the troubled expression carved into Corrigan's face. Slowly it dawned upon him as well that everything they needed was now in the hands of Iron Eyes.

'We'll have to go back down there, Joe,' Lane said. 'Iron Eyes has to be killed. We won't last too long once the sun rises.'

Corrigan nodded. 'I know. That critter only has to stay where he is and wait for us to get thirsty and then he can kill us as easy as swatting a fly.'

Lane was about to speak again when he spotted flames licking up the side of the wagon. Panic carved his face as he gasped in alarm.

'Look,' he yelled.

Corrigan turned on his knees. 'Fire.

Iron Eyes has set my wagon alight, Bob.'

They both watched helplessly as the flames raced up the sides of the wagon canvas. Within seconds the tinder-dry vehicle was engulfed in a fiery inferno. Corrigan watched in horror knowing that neither of them could do anything but watch as his vital supplies burned.

The entire canyon was illuminated by the massive flames which rose thirty feet above the stationary wagon.

'That stinking bounty hunter.' Corrigan spat.

Then he saw the black shape of the gaunt bounty hunter race from the cover of the wagon to his waiting horse.

Corrigan raised his rifle and fired. The shot carved down through the smoke but did not even come close to hitting its well-shielded target.

Iron Eyes reached his stallion and threw himself up on to the hand-tooled saddle. As one shot after another rained down from the caves the bounty hunter turned his mount and spurred hard.

The palomino galloped around the blazing wagon into the array of rocks.

Only after both men had lost sight of the elusive rider did they cease firing their weapons. As both men started to reload their guns and rifle the wagon erupted like a volcano.

The wagon was blown into a million fragments. The entire canyon rocked as fiery mushroom clouds exploded one after another from the blackened cinders.

Shock waves powerfully knocked both Lane and Corrigan off their feet. Burning debris was everywhere. It fell like rain. The canyon was alight with smouldering pieces of wood of every size. Lumps of burning fragments even landed in the cave where Corrigan and Lane had taken refuge.

Corrigan scrambled off his back and raced to the sticks of dynamite. He pulled them away from the burning debris and then stared into the cave's far wall.

Something had caught his eye. The

flickering of the flames lit up the end wall of the cave tunnel. Corrigan stood and stared at it and raised his hand to point.

'Look at the wall, Bob,' he said eagerly. 'Look at it.'

Lane forced himself upright and plucked his guns up off the ground. He stared at the glittering golden wall and moved to Corrigan's shoulder.

'Is that what I think it is?' he gasped.

Corrigan slowly nodded. 'It sure is.'

'Gold?'

'Yep, it's gold.' Corrigan sighed. 'I've searched half the damn caves in this canyon and it was here all the time. We're rich, Bob.'

Lane grabbed the sleeve of his paymaster and stared back at the cave entrance.

'Ain't you forgotten about something, Joe?' he asked as the last of the burning embers were extinguished.

Corrigan realized what Lane meant. He clenched a fist and punched it into the palm of his other hand.

'Iron Eyes,' Corrigan said angrily as he swung on his heels. 'Ain't no point in us sitting on a fortune whilst that bastard is still alive and waiting down there to kill us, Bob.'

'What'll we do?'

Corrigan marched back to the sticks of dynamite and then looked at Lane. A cruel smile etched his face.

'We gotta lure that critter up here and blow his stinking hide to bits,' Corrigan answered. 'And I know exactly how to do it.'

'How?' Lane pressed.

'Pick up that dynamite and follow me, Bob,' Corrigan ordered. 'I'll teach Iron Eyes that it don't pay to tangle with Joe Corrigan.'

12

Joe Corrigan left the cave with Lane close on his heels. Both men ran across the seemingly endless ledge past a dozen or more other cave entrances. Corrigan fired his Winchester down towards the dying embers of the burnt-out wagon. As they reached one of the cave mouths Corrigan stopped and rested his rifle against his hip and blasted the last few bullets down into the canyon as Lane ran into the dark interior with his deadly cargo of explosives.

'Are you in, Bob?' Corrigan shouted over his shoulder as he tossed the rifle aside and drew one of his guns.

Lane was kneeling just inside the cave. 'I'm in the cave, Joe.'

Corrigan spun on his heels and followed his hired gun into the darkness. He crouched beside his shaking companion and stared out into the darkness.

'Why didn't Iron Eyes shoot back?' Lane asked the sweating Corrigan.

'I don't know,' the outlaw replied as he pulled the spent casings from his gun and quickly replaced them. 'Maybe he figures that if he starts shooting we'll know where he's hiding.'

Although neither man would admit it, they were both scared by the infamous bounty hunter. Corrigan holstered his gun and rested his hands on his knees as he studied the canyon carefully.

After the massive explosion and blinding inferno of flame, the canyon was returning to its normal dark self once more. Corrigan looked down from the cave at the diminishing light and the returning shadows. All that remained of the blazing prairie schooner was a few metal hoops set amid burning wood fragments.

'I'll kill Iron Eyes for doing that,' Corrigan vowed.

'The shadows are growing longer, Joe,' Lane commented as he laid the fused dynamite down carefully before them. 'Iron Eyes is waiting for the last of the small fires to go out before he makes his move.'

Corrigan snorted like a bull.

'Yeah, Bob,' he agreed. 'That bounty hunter ain't just brave, he's also cunning.'

'What do you mean?' Lane asked.

'He's like an Injun,' Corrigan added. 'He don't just fight folks. He tries to unsettle the critters he's hunting.'

Lane thought about the way Iron Eyes had fought back at Cheyenne Falls. Every word that Corrigan had said was true. The scrawny bounty hunter did manage to put his prey on the wrong foot somehow.

'Damn it all. I never thought about it before, but you're dead right, Joe.' Lane nodded. 'Everyone that sets eyes on his ugly face is so sick by the sight of him they get themselves killed. Right now he's trying to scare us.'

'He don't scare me.'

'But he's made you angry, Joe,' Lane said. 'When a man gets angry he don't tend to think straight.'

Corrigan glanced briefly at Lane. 'You're right. I am angry, but he don't know that I already got me a plan.'

Just as Corrigan finished talking he spotted the gaunt figure move from what was left of the wagon. Before the outlaw could aim his smoking gun Iron Eyes had disappeared again in the clouds of smoke.

'Iron Eyes is down there close to our horses.' Corrigan spat as he pointed down into the smoke-filled canyon. 'He's closing in on us real slow.'

Lane looked terrified. 'What are we gonna do?'

'Don't go fretting none,' Corrigan said. 'Like I told you, I got me a plan.'

Lane started to believe his cohort. 'What kinda plan?'

'We're gonna kill Iron Eyes, Bob.' Corrigan smiled as he picked up some of the dynamite and shook it under the younger man's nose. 'We're gonna blow him to hell.'

'How?'

Corrigan knew exactly where to place the deadly dynamite sticks and started to string them around the outside of the mouth of the cave entrance. When he had only one stick remaining he patted the arm of his cohort.

'Follow me,' he commanded.

Bob Lane did exactly as he was ordered and trailed Corrigan deeper into the cave tunnel before stopping. Lane could not see a thing.

'Where in tarnation are we going, Joe?' Lane asked fearfully. 'If them sticks of dynamite explode we're trapped in here. Trapped like rats.'

Corrigan did not say a word. He tucked the last stick in the back pocket of his pants and then scratched a match down the cave wall. The small eruption of light flickered as a slight breeze caught its flame. With Lane following on his heels, Corrigan moved through another well-hidden tunnel and only paused to ram the stick of explosives just above the natural cleft in the rock.

'I don't understand,' Lane admitted as he watched Corrigan drop the spent match and immediately strike another one. The shimmering light of the match lit up both of their faces.

'We're gonna make sure that Iron Eyes enters the cave,' he explained. 'When we have that bounty hunter inside the tunnel we shoot at the sticks I planted at the mouth of the cave. Savvy?'

Lane shook his head. 'It ain't gonna work, Joe. Even if he's trapped behind a wall of rock he can escape through here the same way as we're doing.'

Corrigan raised his arm and touched the long fuse dangling from the dynamite stick with his match flame. The fuse started to spit like an angry rattler.

'What are you doing?'

'Iron Eyes can't escape this way, Bob.' Corrigan grinned as he watched the fuse slowly reduce in length. 'This is gonna be just a wall of solid rubble in a few minutes. Iron Eyes will be trapped in the cave tunnel for eternity. This will be the tomb of Iron Eyes.'

Lane nodded. 'It'll be our grave if we don't high-tail it out of here.'

Corrigan led his nervous friend through the strange maze of tunnels until they reached another cave entrance twenty feet away from the one they had entered a few moments before.

The two men lay on their bellies and stared through the eerie darkness along the ridge which linked the entrances of more than a score of caves.

Lane crawled on his belly and squinted over the rim of the ledge. The canyon was still filled with the smoke that floated from the burning wreckage of the wagon.

'Can you see him?' Corrigan asked through gritted teeth.

'Not yet.' Lane rubbed the dirt from his face.

The rocks beneath them shook

violently. A massive cloud of rolling white dust spewed from the cave as the dynamite stick exploded. The entire canyon wall rocked.

Lane turned and was about to crawl back to Corrigan when he saw the dark shadow move from boulder to boulder as the venomous Iron Eyes raced towards the steep slope. Lane scrambled into the cave beside Corrigan.

'I seen him, Joe. He's coming.' Lane trembled.

'Good. Iron Eyes has swallowed the bait.' Corrigan drew his guns and pulled back on their hammers with his thumbs. He lay in the shadows and waited. 'Don't go shooting until I do. Remember we ain't trying to shoot that devilish bastard. We're gonna let him rush into the cave and then we shoot at the dynamite I rigged up.'

Bob Lane fearfully nodded as his shaking hands drew his own guns. Every sinew of his rancid soul wanted to listen to Corrigan, but his frayed nerves told him that Iron Eyes would surely kill them if he had a chance.

'OK, Joe. I'll not start shooting until you say,' Lane reluctantly agreed. 'As long as you're sure that your plan will work.'

'It'll work.' Corrigan grinned. 'He's swallowed my bait and is headed straight for the cave just like I planned. He saw us enter and then there was the explosion. He reckons we're dead but he has to see for himself.'

Lane smiled.

'Curiosity killed the cat,' he said.

'Listen to them spurs,' Corrigan whispered. 'Have you ever heard a cat so curious, Bob?'

'Nope.'

Both secreted men listened to the haunting sound of spurs as Iron Eyes raced up through the swirling clouds of dust and blinding smoke towards the cave. Neither of them had ever seen so much smoke as it continued to pour out of the cave.

A fiendish grin etched across the face

of Corrigan as his hands held both of his six-shooters in readiness.

'Keep on running, Iron Eyes,' he snarled.

13

Choking smoke billowed from the cave mouth and rolled over the edge of the ridge. Neither Corrigan nor his cohort could see anything clearly from where they were hidden. Yet they could both hear the sound of the spurs as they cleared the rim and entered the lethally rigged cave entrance. With the sound of Iron Eyes's spurs jangling in his ears, Corrigan sprang to his feet.

'He's in the cave, Bob,' Corrigan said. 'He's swallowed the bait.'

The deadly outlaw narrowed his eyes and raised both of his guns and took careful aim. He fired four times at the sticks of dynamite which were suspended just above the top of the cave. Lane moved to his side and fired his own gun, but could not see their target as choking dust continued to wash over them.

Then as both ruthless outlaws fanned their gun hammers the entire face of the rocks suddenly exploded. Another three blasts followed in quick succession. Boulders crashed down over the ledge as the deafening vibrations shook the canyon wall.

Corrigan found himself stunned and flat on his back beside Lane. Both men were dazed as they crawled back to their feet and waited for the dust to clear so they could see their deadly handiwork.

Finally after what seemed like a lifetime of waiting the dust cleared and revealed the total destruction they had created.

There was no cave entrance any longer. There was just a massive pile of rubble produced by the explosions. Corrigan rubbed the dust from his face and started to laugh as he approached the shattered rocks.

He turned and looked at Lane and chuckled. 'Now we can go back to that cave down yonder and start digging that wall of gold we found, Bob.'

Lane shook his head. His ears were ringing like a herd of church bells.

Corrigan climbed up on to the rocks and gestured with his arms at the rubble-covered cave mouth. He laughed out loud and took a victorious bow.

'May I present the last resting place of the bounty hunter known as Iron Eyes?' he joked. 'This is the tomb of Iron Eyes.'

Lane was about to join in the celebrations when his blood suddenly ran cold. He began to shake as his dust-filled eyes noticed the tall unmistakable shape of Iron Eyes rise from the slope with his Navy Colts gripped in his bony hands. One gun was aimed at the back of Corrigan whilst the other was trained on Lane.

'Joe?' Lane's shaking voice tried to warn Corrigan that his victory celebrations were a tad premature. 'Listen to me, Joe.'

Corrigan reluctantly stemmed his laughter and stared down from the rocks he was standing upon at the alarmed features of Lane.

'What's wrong with you?' he asked as the starlit shadow of the bounty hunter suddenly spread out across the boulders he was standing upon.

Lane somehow found the courage to raise his guns. It was a pointless act. Before he could pull on his triggers Iron Eyes squeezed one of his own triggers and sent a perfectly aimed shot into the chest of the hired gunman. Lane flew up in the air and crashed on to the rocks.

Corrigan tilted his head and watched as the guns fell from Lane's lifeless hands.

'Bob?' the outlaw called out.

Blood trailed from the hideous wound.

Corrigan watched the starlight dance on the blood which spread away from Lane's chest. He swallowed hard and gripped the guns in his hands firmly. His eyes stared at the long starlit shadow that trailed over the rocks at his feet.

'So you ain't dead, Iron Eyes,' the

outlaw snarled as his eyes watched the shadow moving carefully across the rim until the infamous bounty hunter was facing him. 'I thought I heard you running into the cave.'

The mane of long black hair hung before the scarred face of the bounty hunter as his icy stare watched the outlaw carefully.

'You heard me throwing my spurs into the cave, Corrigan,' Iron Eyes explained coldly as he held his Navy Colts in his bony hands. 'I reckoned on you having a trap figured out. When you heard my spurs hit the cave floor you executed your trap.'

Corrigan felt his trigger fingers twitching against the steel finger guards of his guns. He bit his lower lip and shrugged.

'I've discovered a wall of gold back there in one of the caves, Iron Eyes,' he told the bounty hunter. 'Half of it is yours if you spare my life.'

Iron Eyes shook his head. 'I can't do that.'

Corrigan ventured closer. 'What you mean? We could be partners. There's a fortune in that cave. More than enough for both of us.'

'I like my gold to be minted into golden eagles, Corrigan,' Iron Eyes drawled.

'Then take it all,' Corrigan ranted feverishly. 'Just let me go.'

Iron Eyes shook his head again. 'You're wanted dead or alive, Corrigan. That means I gotta kill you.'

'You're crazy,' Corrigan shouted at the haunting figure. 'I ain't worth a fraction of the fortune in gold that's in that cave yonder.'

Iron Eyes did not say another word. He stood with his guns beside his long thin legs and watched his prey through the limp strands of hair which hung before his bullet-coloured eyes.

'Damn you, Iron Eyes,' Corrigan screamed, and raised both his guns.

As the ruthless outlaw fired both smoking weapons, the bounty hunter turned sideways and raised his left hand until it was level with his shoulder.

Both bullets passed to either side of Iron Eyes's head. The bounty hunter felt their heat burn his skin. His razor-sharp teeth gritted.

Iron Eyes fired.

Corrigan buckled as a bullet tore into his chest. He tried to fire again, but Iron Eyes blasted another merciless shot into him. The outlaw fell to his knees. His guns slid from his hands as his glazed eyes stared at his executioner.

'Why did you kill me, Iron Eyes?' Corrigan spluttered. 'I offered you a fortune and you still killed me. Why?'

'You're wanted, Corrigan,' Iron Eyes sighed.

'What?' Corrigan grabbed the leg of the bounty hunter and pulled the Bowie knife from its hiding place. The wounded outlaw vainly tried to stab the tall figure.

'You're wanted dead or alive,' Iron Eyes whispered before finishing the job with one final bullet. Before the gunsmoke had drifted away from the outlaw, Iron Eyes snatched his knife out of Corrigan's dead grip and returned it to his boot neck. 'In my book that means only dead.'

Iron Eyes pushed his guns into the deep pockets of his trail coat. His bony hand reached down, grabbed Corrigan's blood-soaked collar and lifted the limp corpse up off the sand. Iron Eyes dragged the lifeless carcass down the slope towards the horses.

The emotionless bounty hunter hauled the valuable body to where Lane's saddle mount was tethered. He lifted the dead weight up and grabbed it around the middle. Mustering every scrap of his strength, Iron Eyes slid it on to the mount's saddle. He sighed and then used the cutting rope to secure it.

'That ought to hold you,' he snarled.

Rubbing the blood from his hands down his coat front, Iron Eyes grabbed the reins. He silently led the horse on towards the desert. Iron Eyes paused close to the ashes of the wagon as his palomino stallion wandered out of the smoke towards its master. The haunting eyes of the emaciated bounty hunter watched as the powerful horse stopped beside him.

'I'm glad you hung around,' Iron Eyes told the handsome animal before grabbing the ornate saddle horn.

In one fluid action the bounty hunter mounted the high-shouldered horse. He tied the reins of the mount carrying Corrigan's body to his cantle and paused for a moment as his eyes looked up at the caves.

'So there's a wall of gold up there?' He repeated the outlaw's claims and then produced a cigar and rammed it into the corner of his mouth. 'Who gives a damn?'

Iron Eyes struck a match across his silver saddle horn and cupped its flame. He inhaled deeply and tossed his mane of black hair from his hideous features. Smoke drifted from his teeth as he went to jab the flesh of his horse. He looked down at his mule-eared boots and then back at the dead body he had in tow.

'At least your bounty will buy me some new spurs, you bastard,' he said before slapping the lengths of his long reins across the tail of his mount.

The haunting figure of Iron Eyes sat astride his powerful stallion as the animal started across the arid starlit desert back towards distant Cheyenne Falls. As the stallion gathered pace, Iron Eyes looked over his shoulder at the dead outlaw's body atop the saddle horse he was towing. A satisfied smirk etched the scarred face as his teeth gripped the long black cigar firmly.

'Reckon I should reach the town and collect the bounty on this varmint just about sunrise,' Iron Eyes said as smoke drifted from his teeth over the carcass behind him. His eyes narrowed as he glanced at what was left of Joe Corrigan. 'Sorry about spoiling your plans, but I ain't ready to be buried in no tomb just yet.'

Iron Eyes increased his pace and drove the stallion over the sand; his aim was to reach Cheyenne Falls before sunrise. He did not wish to be caught out in the desert when the merciless sun returned to the cloudless sky.

14

It was a few hours before dawn when the townsfolk of Cheyenne Falls who were still awake heard the familiar noise of an approaching stagecoach; the noise echoed off the buildings within the boundaries of their remote settlement, yet there were no stagecoaches due for another two days.

Rattling chains and pounding hoofs awoke Sheriff Cord from his deep slumber. His wrinkled eyes looked around his small office as he realized that yet again he had forgotten to go home. He listened to the clattering of muscular horses in their traces and the cracking of a bullwhip and then rose from his swivel chair and walked to the wide-open doorway.

It was still dark.

'What the hell is the time?' Cord yawned.

He rested a hand upon the door-frame and stared out into the amber street light and listened to the sound of quickly rotating wheels growing louder as the stagecoach driver expertly negotiated the twisting streets. His knuckles rubbed the sleep from his eyes before he glanced at the wall calendar and that day's date, which had yet to be crossed out with the pencil hanging nearby on a string.

'Now that's odd,' Cord muttered to himself before he pulled his pipe from his vest pocket and tapped his teeth with its stem. 'The stage ain't due for a couple of days yet.'

He screwed up his eyes and looked across at the Overland Stagecoach depot. It was locked up tight. Cord couldn't understand what was going on. If there were a stage due today at this ungodly hour, the depot would be open and its staff would be ready with a fresh team.

'What's going on here?' he asked the moths which fluttered around the lantern that hung from the porch overhang. As the lawman ambled out on to the lantern-lit boardwalk he heard and then saw the stagecoach as it skidded around the corner and began to race into Main Street.

His eyes widened as he watched the six lathered-up horses thunder down the street towards him and his office. The team were fighting against their restraints as they towed the battered stagecoach down the long thoroughfare.

Cord frowned and moved to the edge of the boardwalk.

He could barely believe his eyes. High on the driver's seat sat Squirrel Sally looking as if she were made of a mixture of caked dust and vicious rage. She lashed the reins down with all her might as her toes rested against the brake pole. Then she spotted the tin star pinned to Cord's vest and aimed her team towards the startled man.

'If I ain't mistaken that's a little gal driving that big old stage,' he muttered as his teeth gripped the pipe and his eyebrows rose above his unblinking eyes.

Squirrel Sally wrapped the hefty reins around her arms and leaned back as her bare foot pushed down on the brake pole. The brakes screeched. A cloud of dust kicked up from the horses' hoofs as they stopped just outside the sheriff's office.

The lawman stared up at the tiny female as she looped the reins around the brake pole and swung her shapely frame from the driver's seat and clambered down over the front wheel.

Sally leaned forwards at the tin star pinned to the lawman's vest and then grabbed the pipe from his lips. Cord was about to object, but she had already scratched a match across her rear and raised the flame over the pipe bowl. She puffed for a few seconds and then ducked under Cord's arm and entered his office.

The befuddled sheriff turned and

followed her. He watched as she filled a tin cup with the last of his coffee and drained it.

'Who the hell are you?' Cord stammered as the petite female paced around the office puffing on the pipe.

She paused and looked at the lawman. 'I'm Squirrel Sally and I've come to find my man. I've also got to save his sorry hide as well.'

Cord was still no clearer. 'You ain't gonna find him here, little lady.'

Her eyebrows rose. 'I ain't no lady. I'm Squirrel Sally.'

The sheriff was about to grab her, but thought better of it as she continued to pace around his office thoughtfully. He tried to keep pace with her, then gave up and sat down.

'Have you seen my man?' Sally asked through a cloud of pipe smoke. 'His name's Iron Eyes.'

Josiah Cord looked at her in disbelief.

'You're Iron Eyes's woman?' he gasped at the tiny female.

Sally gave a firm nod and glanced out at the street before returning to the seated lawman. She removed the pipe from her lips and aimed its stem at Cord.

'Have you seen him?' she repeated.

Cord nodded slowly.

Sally spread her legs apart and leaned closer to the veteran lawman. Her head tilted as she studied his face.

'You have? Good. Where the hell is that long streak of bacon? I gotta tell him something real curious. Something I overheard in Coleman City. Where is he?'

Cord raised his hands as if in surrender.

'Stop gabbing so fast, young 'un. I can't think as fast as you can talk,' he said.

The small female straightened up and hitched her pants up before resting her knuckles on her hips.

'I've done gabbing and you still ain't said nothing, old-timer,' she snorted. 'I'm waiting.'

'Waiting for what?' Cord stammered nervously.

She leaned forward. Her face was nearly pressed against his. 'I'm waiting for you to answer my questions. Where's my betrothed? Tell me where Iron Eyes is.'

Josiah Cord leaned back in his hardback chair, but the further back he leant the more she pressed her face into his face. He went to raise his hands and push her off him, but then his eyes noticed that her frayed skin-tight shirt was missing most of its buttons. His eyes gratefully focused on her firm breasts. He lowered his shaking hands and gripped the wooden chair instead.

'Iron Eyes left town,' he somehow managed to say.

Sally stood bolt upright. 'He left?'

Sheriff Cord nodded sheepishly. 'He went after an outlaw called Joe Corrigan. There were five gunmen in town and they tried to kill Iron Eyes.'

'Where are these varmints now?'

Sally puffed on the lawman's pipe again.

'All but one of them are dead,' Cord told her. 'Your man killed them.'

Squirrel Sally looked down at the lawman in surprise. 'One of them is still alive?'

Cord nodded. 'He lit out and Iron Eyes saddled that fine palomino stallion of his and followed. He reckoned the hired killer would lead him to Joe Corrigan. There's bounty on Corrigan.'

She smiled proudly. 'Iron Eyes is darn smart and no mistake.'

'How come you're so anxious to talk with him, Squirrel?' Cord asked as he adjusted himself in the unforgiving chair.

Her face suddenly looked grim. She returned the pipe to the lawman's mouth and shook her tired head.

'Some critter in town called Bevis wired a gunfighter that Iron Eyes was in Cheyenne Falls. He told this critter, Drako Sharp, to get here as fast as possible,' she explained.

The sheriff held his pipe in his teeth and looked at the troubled female. He rose up and tried to look at her face, but she turned away.

'Bevis runs the hotel down the street yonder, gal,' Cord told her. 'I ain't got no idea why he'd send for a gunfighter or why he'd want to tell the varmint about Iron Eyes.'

Suddenly Squirrel Sally was no longer upset. She was angry. Her eyes flashed up into the concerned face of the lawman as a wicked smile came to her lips.

'So Bevis runs the hotel, huh?' she repeated.

Cord nodded. 'Yep.'

Sally did not utter another word. She ran from the office and jumped up on to the stagecoach wheel. She stretched and hauled her trusty Winchester from the driver's seat and then jumped back down on to the weathered boardwalk.

As Josiah Cord emerged back out into the night air he watched as her small hands cocked the rifle's hand guard. A spent bullet casing bounced off his chest.

'What you doing?' he asked her.

Sally did not say a word as she checked her rifle was fully loaded.

Cord recognized the look in her beautiful dust-caked face. It was the look of determination. He lunged forward and tried to stop her, but Sally was too agile and avoided him. Her bare feet skipped off the boardwalk as she headed for the hotel.

'What are you going to do, Sally gal?' Cord shouted.

She looked back through her blonde curls at the lawman and smiled broadly.

'I'm going to the hotel,' she shouted back.

'Yeah, but what for?' the sheriff asked.

Sally patted her rifle.

'To get me some answers.' She smiled.

'What if Bevis don't give you any answers?' Sheriff Cord asked nervously.

'He'll answer me,' Sally said. 'Either

that or he'll die.'

Ben Bevis was standing in the porch
light of his hotel. He too had heard the
sound of the bullet-scarred stagecoach
as it had been driven into Cheyenne
Falls. Now he was watching the small
female as she homed in on him with her
rifle clutched in her tiny hands.
Although he had no reason to be afraid
of the unknown girl, Bevis suddenly
caught a glimpse of her determined
features as she walked beneath a street
light.

The hotelier felt nervous. He had
seen many faces over the years and
recognized the expression upon Sally's
dust-caked face.

Sweat defied the temperature and
rolled down his face as she got closer.
Her beautiful eyes were trained on him
as if he was the only other living soul
within the confines of the sprawling
town.

Bevis lowered his hand from the
wooden upright and rubbed its sweaty
palm down his jacket tail. He wanted to

run, but could not imagine why.

Then as Sally got within thirty feet of the hotel she stopped, cocked her rifle and fired. The shot ripped through the padded shoulder of Bevis's jacket.

Bevis staggered backward as smouldering cotton fibre floated all around him. He raised a hand as if in defence and stared at Sally.

'Who the hell are you?' Bevis shouted. 'What are you shooting at me for? I ain't done anything.'

She began to approach Bevis again. Her rifle stock was resting against her groin. Smoke trailed from its long-gleaming barrel as she frowned at him. She stepped up on to the boardwalk outside the hotel door with her trusty Winchester aimed at his guts. Sally stopped.

'What are you doing?' Bevis waved his hands at her. 'I've not done anything.'

Squirrel Sally tilted her handsome head back and looked into the face of Bevis. There was a hint of amusement in her face as she cocked the rifle again. The sight of panic in his face encouraged her closer.

'You know why I'm here,' she blurted out as her rifle pressed into his girth. 'You sent for some dude named Drako Sharp and I wanna know why.'

Ben Bevis looked terrified. It might have been the cold steel of her weapon or it could have been the expression on her otherwise cute face.

His eyes darted back and forth in a pitiful bid to find someone who could help him. He saw Sheriff Cord down the long street as the lawman puffed on his pipe. It seemed to Bevis that even the sheriff was afraid of the mysterious female. He looked down at her and tried to smile.

'How do you know about Drako?' Bevis asked. 'Nobody knows about my sending for Drako.'

'Liar.' Squirrel Sally forced Bevis up against the wall of the hotel. 'I was in Coleman City when your telegraph message arrived, Bevis. Why did you tell a gunfighter that Iron Eyes was in Cheyenne Falls?'

The lantern light cast its amber hue over his sweating head as she pressed the rifle barrel deeper into his belly. His eyes stared down at the furious face below him.

'A long time ago I tangled with Iron Eyes,' Bevis admitted. 'He didn't recognize me when he registered in my hotel, but I knew it was only a matter of time before he would and then I'd be a dead man.'

'What's this Drako Sharp critter gotta do with all this?' Sally hissed. 'Why would you be sending for a hired gunfighter?'

Bevis closed his eyes in anticipation of the worst. 'OK, I admit it. I wired Drako to come and kill Iron Eyes.'

Squirrel Sally was about to pull the trigger when she heard footsteps behind her. She refused to turn around and imagined it was the old sheriff.

'Leave me be, Sheriff,' she riled. 'This bastard deserves killing and I'm not gonna disappoint him.'

Abruptly a gun barrel was smashed across the back of her head. She stumbled forward and fell into a heap at the feet of the terrified Bevis. His eyes looked up at the gunfighter and gave a grateful nod.

'It's about time you showed, Drako,' Bevis sighed.

Drako Sharp looked down at the female as he returned his bloodstained gun to its holster. His eyes then glanced over his shoulder at the unconscious lawman, who had also succumbed to his brutal beating.

'Where's Iron Eyes?' Sharp asked.

'He'll be back here soon enough,' Bevis replied.

'I'll go and drag that sheriff off to his office and lock him up while we wait,' Sharp drawled as he turned and started to walk back along the street to where Cord lay in a pool of his own blood. 'We don't want that old critter waking up before the bounty hunter gets back here, do we?'

Bevis stepped over Squirrel Sally to the side of the deadly hired gunfighter. He grabbed Sharp's arm and pointed back at the motionless female. 'What about her? Maybe we should lock her up in the sheriff's office as well.'

Sharp paused and looked back at Sally. An even smile etched his unshaven features.

'I've got other plans for her, Bevis,' he said lustfully. 'She's gonna make me real happy after I dispatch Iron Eyes to Boot Hill.'

Less than an hour later the black sky was transformed into a glowing panorama of golden light. The sun was about to rise when the morning silence was broken by the sound of horses walking into the streets of Cheyenne Falls.

Two horses with very different burdens.

The palomino stallion carried its master whilst the saddle horse was weighed down by the body of Joe Corrigan slumped over its saddle.

The bounty hunter had timed his arrival to perfection. He had beaten the sun to Cheyenne Falls and brought his dead cargo back. Iron Eyes was slumped over his saddle horn as he reached the sheriff's office.

Iron Eyes turned the head of the powerful stallion towards the hitching rail and water trough. He looped his long thin leg over the animal's milky mane and slid to the ground.

As he tied his reins to the hitching pole he sensed that something was wrong in Cheyenne Falls. Years of travelling in search of his next prey had heightened his senses. He looked down at the churned-up sand and saw the deep wheel tracks.

'Only a stagecoach could have left them marks,' he said as his bullet-coloured eyes followed the tracks. 'A stagecoach which has been taken off the street and hidden for some reason.'

He rubbed his chin and thought about Squirrel Sally. Could she have trailed him to this town? Had her stagecoach left those tracks?

Iron Eyes stared over the ornate saddle. The town was mysteriously empty of people going about their daily business.

Without even realizing it, his bony right hand slid one of his Navy Colts from his deep coat pocket. He cocked the gun's hammer and gripped it firmly as he stepped up on to the boardwalk and tried the office door.

To his surprise, it was locked. Iron Eyes turned and surveyed the empty street again. He knew that there was only one reason why a town's inhabitants remained indoors when the sun was up.

They were too scared to venture out.

Iron Eyes thought about the stagecoach again. He knew full well that there was only one reason to hide it. Someone did not want him to know that Squirrel was somewhere in town.

He ran his long fingers through his hair and looked along the street to the hotel. He recalled the message Ben

Bevis had wired to Drako Sharp the day before and started to nod to himself knowingly.

That was it, he thought.

The gunfighter had arrived in Cheyenne Falls and was somewhere waiting to earn his blood money. Iron Eyes started to walk slowly along the boardwalk towards the hotel as he tried to bring to mind where he had seen Bevis before.

He had always prided himself on the fact that he never forgot a name or the face of a man who was wanted dead or alive. He stepped down and crossed to the boardwalk outside the shuttered barber's shop and had only just placed a boot upon its weathered surface when his razor-sharp memory gave him the answer he sought.

'His name ain't Bevis,' Iron Eyes said as he scratched a match down a porch upright and lit his last cigar. 'It's Ben White and he's wanted dead or alive.'

A satisfied smirk was suddenly wiped from his scarred face as his keen eyes noticed a figure tied up outside the hotel. He rushed forward and realized that the figure was that of his feisty friend.

'Squirrel,' he shouted angrily. He dragged the cigar from his mouth and tossed it at the sand. His narrowed eyes focused on the limp female as she hung by her wrists from the hotel façade. Her head was slumped forward. He could not tell if she was alive or dead.

With no thought for his own safety Iron Eyes leapt down from the boardwalk and ran towards her. Without warning, a shot came from his right. He felt its impact as the bullet ripped through his sleeve and grazed his arm. He staggered as his gun fell from his hand.

Iron Eyes hit the sand and rolled over until he was braced on his knees. His eyes darted around the street until they spotted a trail of gunsmoke drifting on the air.

Then Iron Eyes saw him.

The tall figure of Drako Sharp

appeared with both his guns in his hands. One had smoke trailing from its barrel as the man squared up to Iron Eyes like a matador facing a deadly bull.

'So you're the legendary Iron Eyes?' Sharp mocked. 'You don't look so dangerous to me. Hell, you ain't nothing but a hideous skeleton.'

The bounty hunter got back to his feet and glanced back at his gun on the sand. He then exhaled and glared at the gunfighter.

'And you must be Drako Sharp,' he said as his eyes spotted the familiar figure of Ben Bevis standing in the hotel lobby doorway.

'You heard of me?' Sharp asked.

'Yep.' Iron Eyes dipped his left hand into his trail-coat pocket and slid his index finger around the trigger of his other Navy Colt. 'I've heard about you.'

'What you heard?' Sharp wondered.

Iron Eyes drew his gun from his pocket and fanned its hammer three times. He watched as the gunfighter dropped on to his knees and then fell face first into the sand. He walked towards the dead gunfighter and looked down upon him.

'I lied,' he said.

Then faster than the blink of an eye he turned, raised the gun and fired at the hotel lobby. Ben Bevis staggered out of the open doorway with a rifle in his hands.

Iron Eyes fanned his hammer again and watched as Bevis was lifted off his feet by his deadly shot and knocked into the hotel lobby. Blood trailed his body to its resting place.

No sooner had Bevis collided with the floorboards than the bounty hunter started running towards Squirrel Sally. He reached her unconscious form, wrapped his arm around her and cut the ropes which secured her wrists, with his Bowie knife.

Iron Eyes caught her dead weight in his arms and cradled her as if she was a cherished infant. She slumped into him.

Finale

Iron Eyes sat on the steps of the hotel boardwalk and frantically patted her cheek with his skeletal fingers.

'Wake up, Squirrel,' he urged her desperately. 'Wake up, gal. You can't die on old Iron Eyes.'

He looked at her face. For the first time he realized how beautiful it was. He rubbed the dust from her cheeks and patted them again feverishly. She still showed no sign of being alive.

Iron Eyes stood and turned. He laid her down on her back and placed his ear against her chest. To his surprise he heard her heart beating like a war drum. He lifted his head up and saw her eyes flutter and open. Relief washed over him.

She stared at him and then lifted her head off the boardwalk and studied her torn shirt and exposed breasts. Her eyebrows lifted.

'What you bin doing to me, Iron Eyes?' she suggested.

The bounty hunter was surprised and embarrassed.

'I never did anything. I was just checking to see if you were alive, Squirrel,' he stammered.

She grabbed both sides of his coat lapels and dragged his face down towards her own. 'Admit it. You've bin playing with my chests again. That's it, ain't it? You realize this means we're married, don't you?'

The bounty hunter swallowed hard. 'What?'

Squirrel Sally tugged on his lapels and kissed him long and hard. Iron Eyes pulled himself free. He was flustered and then noticed that the female was laughing at him. He frowned and pointed a finger at her.

'You trouble me, Squirrel,' he announced. 'I thought you were dead.'

Squirrel Sally sat upright and rubbed

her skinned wrists as she watched him fondly.

'Were you sad when you thought I was dead, Iron Eyes?' she asked. 'Were you?'

Iron Eyes picked his gun off the sand and looked into her blue eyes. He shrugged and raised an eyebrow. 'What the hell do you think, Squirrel?'

We do hope that you have enjoyed reading this large print book.

Did you know that all of our titles are available for purchase?

We publish a wide range of high quality large print books including:
Romances, Mysteries, Classics
General Fiction
Non Fiction and Westerns

Special interest titles available in large print are:
The Little Oxford Dictionary
Music Book, Song Book
Hymn Book, Service Book

Also available from us courtesy of Oxford University Press:
Young Readers' Dictionary
(large print edition)
Young Readers' Thesaurus
(large print edition)

For further information or a free brochure, please contact us at:
Ulverscroft Large Print Books Ltd.,
The Green, Bradgate Road, Anstey,
Leicester, LE7 7FU, England.
Tel: (00 44) 0116 236 4325
Fax: (00 44) 0116 234 0205

TWO FROM TEXAS

Neil Hunter

One of the men arrives in Gunner Creek at the end of a long search, whilst the other simply drifts into the town. Fate has drawn them together: two Texans who find a town in trouble — and, being who they were, have to throw in their hands to help. Chet Ballard and Jess McCall are Texicans down to the tips of their boots. Big men with hard fists and fast guns, who see trouble and refuse to back away from it . . .

DERBY JOHN'S ALIBI

Ethan Flagg

Derby John Daggert is out for revenge on his employer after a severe beating meted out for theft and adultery. Then a robbery goes badly wrong, two men are murdered, and the killer makes a wild ride from Querida to Denver. As prime suspect, Daggert is arrested, but his lawyer convinces the jury he was elsewhere when the crime was committed. It is left to Buckskin Joe Swann to hunt down the culprit — a task more difficult than he could have ever imagined . . .

HOOD

Jake Douglas

When he wakes wounded in the badlands, he doesn't even know his own name, where he is, or how he got there. He sure doesn't know who shot him and left him to die. But when the riders come to try and finish the job, they call him 'Hood' ... Under the scorching sun, he does the only thing he can: straps on a six-gun, gets back in the saddle, and sets out to find out who's on his trail ...